The N.M.E.

THE N.M.E.

A NOVEL IN VERSE BY

RYAN A. KOVACS

PHiR Publishing
San Antonio

PHiR Publishing
San Antonio, TX
phirpublishing.com

Second edition: March 2022

ISBN 978-1-7370627-5-2
LCCN 2021925592

Printed in the United States of America

This book is dedicated to my supportive wife, Emma and my encouraging mother, Julie. These two women have been the push at my back when I wanted to give up, my reassurance when I was filled with doubt and above all, my true believers when I had no faith in myself. I love you both. Thank you for always being there for me.

"Revenge is a confession of pain."
—Latin Proverb

BRUNO

Bruno

was a man
that some would call legend
others'd call an imposter.

he was not real
an'
he was not fake.

he was a man
who, when born
did not cry
for, he wasn't afraid of this
ugly world.

who, when growin' up
contradicted the phrase
'growin' like a weed.'

in fact
Bruno
was the definition
of his own name.

When he was 11

he had his first taste'a
blood
when he were on the
home plate playin' ball.

his first swing'a the season
he gone'n hit a bird
wit the bat
that flew in t'his left handed swing
as his right leg slipp'd
an' the umpire yelled
"strrrrrrr-ike!"

though he mourned fer the loss
a'that lesser creature
while he pick'd feathers
outta the dry blood caked on the bat
that was the day
that start'd the days t'come.

When he was 15

he drove his first pick-up truck
that he damn stole from his uncle
while he locked'm in his barn
wit the woman he'd not yet married
who tried to go'n be Bruno's mother.

he tied 'em together
with her entrails
an' a few lengths'a barb'd wire
and he didn't wear no gloves.

his uncle screamed
just b'fore Bruno shot'm in the head
with his uncle's own Colt .45
then emptied a can'a gasoline
'round the bodies
an' left it t'burn like the fire in his heart.

When he was 24

Bruno got arrested
fer stealin'
murder
an' arson
and put in t'the facility
many claim
ain't no prison to the body
yet t'the mind.

but Bruno were bigger than the mind.

He stood

at five feet an'
seven inches
towering over
all those shorter than him.

he was as wide as he were tall
standin' as straight
an' as tough
as a rock maple
minus the leaves that'd shed in the fall.

and he never fell.

but, rest assured
if the man fell in the middle'a the damned woods
wit no one there t'hear it

he'd make a fuckin' sound.

His legs

bulged through ev'ry pair'a pants
he attempted t'put on.

jus' the thought of fabric tryin' to
mold t'the muscle structure of his quadriceps
would tear in sheer fear
an' gather at his feet.

they were so powerful
that one time he got his legs 'round
another man's neck
merely flexed fer a moment
an' the man's head shot off like a damn cork
on a '47 Cheval Blanc.

red'n all.

His hands

were so powerful
that he would grab pebbles
an' crush 'em t'make sand.

they were always dirty
an' callused over
t'the point
where if he left a hand print
it would be confused fer'a gorilla.

he always gnawed down his finger nails
b'cause if he made'a fist
and hit someone
the force he'd hit with would push his nails
in t'the palms of his hands
makin'em bleed.

His skin

was as thick as'a rhinoceros
an' as warm as a bottle of Japanese saki
where any insect that attempted t'land
would either fail miserably at
attemptin' to penetrate his epidermis
an' be squashed with his pinkie
or would be plucked outta the air
with his enticin' scent
sendin' the insect spellbound drunk
t'the ground
where the heel of his boot
would end its meaningless life.

His jaw

was chiseled and sculpted
to look like'a rock formation
intended t'be in the grand canyon.
it was there, that he grew a thin beard
which he'd shave his neck every other day
except Friday's
in order t'give him a five a'clock shadow
by noon.
from his left ear t'the base of his chin
he had a scar that looked as though
he were slowly cut with'a dull blade
exposin' his bone
then sewn up after he nearly bled outta his cheek.

His chest

was bulky an' full of matted down hair
minus two nipples
where it was rumored
he had 'em cut off durin' an
interrogation by local authorities
on the whereabouts of his missin'
uncle an' substitute mother of an aunt.

when he'd breathe
his chest'd puff out like one of them
puffer fish attemptin' to scare away other fish
'cept he was not t'be fucked wit
on the exhale.

Bruno was a man

unlike any other man
with balls of steel
and the balls to prove it
that he was above all
the biggest dick
you'd ever have the
misfortune of knowin'.

A few things you ought to know

'bout Bruno's reputation.
he was referred t'as the walkin' mammoth
due to his inability t'feel pain.

he had a temper
wit a fuse, that if ignited
would go off no matter yer gender title'r size.

he would not scream or yell
yet allow his body to work freely with no reaction.

he did not flinch.

he did not stop.

but he was still a man.
don't ya forget it.

Me

I'm jus' a guy
that wants somethin' more from this life.

though I cannot have what was taken from me
I am hell bent'n driven
on obtaining the cause.

an' no person
no obstacle
nor emotion
will stop me
   from killin' my father.

Bruno and I

were pals from the get go
as childhood teen years blended in t'adult years
that faded all the way t'prison.

sharin' a brick'n mortar cell
shitter
an' occasionally the same barbell
in the weight yard.

that was the extent of our
similarities.

what brought us close however
were our diff'rences.

without the obvious size difference
many thought us t'be a duo
of dynamic distaste an' displeasure.

we were the meanest sons'a bitches
an' in'a prison full of prisoners
we took no prisoners
when those who defied us
tried their best
t'best us.

no matter their numbers
no matter their size
no matter their role
Bruno'n I
we stood side by side
like a phalanx
nev'r weary
an' always willing.

Patience

was not my strongest trait
but a trait worth mentionin'
b'cause I've been waitin' fer so long now
to do the only thing left t'do in life.

kill my father.

you might think I got me
some kinda obsession
like them men that lift weights
everyday t'pass time
'er get big.

there they'd be
8:20 n'the a.m. right after
breakfast chow
on the bench
wit them half cut t-shirts
an' pants rolled from the belly button
down t'their hips
for pussy leverage an' appeal
pushin' that bar'n metal t'wards the
big blue sky
on repeat like'a record skippin'
the same verse over'n over.

Them guys

were Bruno's fav'rit to get on about.

he'd laugh like a jackal a'ways from them
pointing his fingers
that gripped his mornin' cig
eggin'em on t'do more
to be men
to grow a pair
to hike up them pants
put their t-shirt sleeves back on
an' then get the fuck off the bench.

One day

Harry was on the bench
big Sasquatch mother-fucker
who lived up t'his name
attemptin' t'push up 180 pound daisies.

took'm two attempts
b'fore he got it up once without assistance
from his bar-holdin' bitch.

Bruno stood 'gainst the brick wall
ridiculin' him an' his weakness.

Harry sat up off the bench
turned his head
"pack of cigs says you can't bench
the whole pallet once you big fuck."

Bruno's face contorted from a
humorous smile to a sly grin
as he cocked his head t'the side
analyzin' the pallet an' challenge.

"how 'bout a pack fer each time
it reaches the sky pal?"
Bruno asked confidently.

"and if you can't get it up?"
Harry teased.

"I owe you a pack fer each ten pounds on the pallet."

Harry laughed eagerly
"you're on
ya damn oaf."

Bruno walked

like the ground below'm were afraid
of his footprint.

his strides were short
an' meaningful
wit a destination in mind.

he did not, under any circumstances
ever run towards somethin'
nor away from nothin' neither
'cause he would become
the biggest juggernaut you'd ever see.

When he reached the bench

at his own pace'a curiosity
mixed with a whole lot'a people
swarmin' the area
he started t'put plates on each side'a the bar
barely breathin' heavy with each one he picked up.

took'm two minutes t'put all eighteen plates
of different sizes an' weights evenly distributed
'cross the bar as it started to bend upwards.

the other inmates hoarded 'round
like some cheap hooker'd come by
an' was givin' free piece a'cunt
wit all sorts of chatter.

bets bein' made—
disputes over how much weight it was—
a number you'd be afraid of I might add—
wit how many thought he'd drop the bar an' crush his chest
or the low chatter below teeth and tobacco
over how many reps he'd do.

Bruno turned t'Harry
"you better pay up you hairy-son-of-a-monkey
or so help me I'll use yer asshole like a slot machine
an' these weights'll be the coins."

"why don't you try'n get the bar up first
you piece'a shit,"
Harry snarled.

His veins were like fault lines

stretchin' from every crevice on his body.

veins so large an' thick
they looked as though night crawlers
had got stuck under his skin
an' were pushin' an' pumpin'
t'burst through with the given chance.

the veins on his arms were rigid an' plump
so juicy an' ripe
a nurse'd have a field day pokin'm.

the vein on the left side-a-his neck was as green
as'a head of lettuce
an' the one on his forehead
swelled and pulsated with each rep he pumped out.

sweat beaded
an' once it got to a vein
unable t'climb over the hump
sought the path'a least resistance
pooling into his unrolled-up pants.

By the time he was finished

Harry owed Bruno a carton'a cigs
plus 3 more packs fer interest
on makin' him wait 'til the next shipment came in.

the courtyard was pretty quiet fer awhile
as some men were puckerin' their ass cheeks
'cause they got raped'n bets
favors and disbelief.

me on the other hand
made out jus' fine'n dandy
since I was the only one bettin' on him makin' it
and callin' the exact number he'd put up.

can't say it was a scam
but a few tried t'claim such unproven accusations
until Bruno showed up an' gave'm a look
that was better than tellin'em t'pay up—
and they all did.

twenty-two cartons
eight boxes
four favors
an' even more enemies than we started out with
ev'ryone were practically persuaded t'stay away from us.

only one that was left t'convince
was easy on the eyes
an' hard on the dick.

THE GIRL

Arlene's legs

were as long an' straight
as most state thruways.

in fact
if you were to try an' trace her
from her feet t'her waist
you'd be prompted t'pay a toll
at her knees.

they glistened under sunlight
from the lotion that she'd lather on
the mornin' of her Tuesday visits
an' all the men would whistle like sirens
and howl like wolves
at the sound'a her tender voice
askin' permission t'enter through the prison gates
jus' b'fore she'd strut in.

she were a shrink
volunteering
t'look good on paper
tacklin' the most troubled minds
on this side-a-the Mississippi.

Most of the men

gave'r sob stories
'bout how they shouldn't be there
or that they didn't commit
whichever crime they'd been accused.
bunch'a white men that'd been found plenty guilty
hoping fer a chance in hell t'get outta jail free.

there was the occasional fool
that would ask fer sexual favors
paid in full wit other sexual favors
an' she'd just write down every thing they said
with'a tilted nod
and an
"okay, that concludes our session today.
thank you."

I heard that Frank went in there once
openin' with the statement
"I wanna lick you
from yer chin to yer lips doll...

the long way."

an' she gave him the notorious line
she gave everyone else b'fore and aft
"okay, that concludes our session today.
thank you."

There was beauty about Arlene

that jus' couldn't be captured by
even a famous painter like
DaVinci or Donatello.

most the boys thought
she were some incarnation
of a delicate desert rose—
that she'd been pluck'd
and plant'd amongst the scum a'this earth
by some divine bein'
so all the men could bathe in'r
soakin' her insides t'make'r flourish.

she coulda been the exception
t'being surrounded by shit
an' still come out smellin' like roses.

Her pale skin caught color

like she were'a blank canvas.
each brush stroke of color
that caressed her smooth face
warned'a flashin' sign of danger
when she'd stand hunched over the sink
glidin' blood red lipstick 'long the crevices
of her lips.

she'd pucker 'em in front'a the mirror
of the men's bathroom with big'ol Johnny Boy
guardin' the door
starin' at her well rounded rump.

I made a pass at her

"no sense in buttering yerself up ma'am.
boys aren't all lookin' at yer face."

Johnny Boy broke his concentration
and stuttered in his speech
"wa...watch your tongue you piece of shit."

he lock'd eyes wit me
"you wanna kiss 'er somethin'?"

he moved a step closer t'me
"get back to yer cell
b'fore I beat you and I have to drag ya back."

"yer the boss.
but if ya could stop standin' in the doorway
the boys'n I would appreciate seein' the show
you seem t'always have front row tickets to."

his face turned red like Arlene's lips
as he pointed in the direction he wanted me t'move
all while Arlene shook her little toosh for me
behind Johnny's back
while all the boys started whistlin'.

Piece of shit

Johnny Boy was no diff'rent than the rest of us in that prison
despite bein' the top-dog guard
'cept he was allowed t'get away wit his insults an' beatings
'cause his daddy was the warden.
Johnny Boy was the kinda guy that'd beat ya
jus' fer lookin' in his general direction.
most'a the men kept their distance
after he damn near killed Floyd
few months prior.

Floyd sneezed on the back'a Johnny's neck
durin' a random search
then turned 'round and cracked Floyd wit his baton
shatterin' his jaw an' sendin' teeth flying
'cross and over the rail on t'Harry below.
blood spewed outta Floyd's mouth
until his face were unrecognizable.
when they drag'd his sorry ass 'cross the floor
t'the infirmary
his face leaked blood on the fading yellow tile
like he were'a pen writin' his last breaths'a life.

Johnny wiped the chunk'a flesh an' blood
from his beater stick
cacklin' t'another guard nearby
"fucker is gonna get me sick now."

guess Johnny Boy didn't know
Floyd had'a fuckin' fear of germs
an' was likely allergic to Johnny's bullshit.

I could feel Johnny's stare on my back

burnin' a hole in my shirt
as the steam from my ears prolly shot out like cannons
from his smug comment.

I felt a soft touch attempt t'squeeze my shoulder
while a voice as big as'a mouse soothed
the pressure in my head
callin' out t'me

"excuse me
Bruno... is it?"

I turned t'look her in the face
"wrong guy ma'am.
he's over yonder."

her look was vacant yet growin' in intensity
as she searched in the direction t'which I'd pointed
"my apologies, Johnny said he was you
must have gotten confused."

"well ma'am, Bruno'n I are always 'round each other
Johnny Boy over there jus' likes t'fuck wit us all
which now apparently includes you too."

Her cheeks began to hue

as her smile remained hidden
while she turned away from me proceedin' t'her office.

after a few steps she paused
like she could feel my stare at her ass
rippin' off her clothes
an' turned t'me
"stop by my office next week
I haven't had the pleasure of speaking to you yet."

"sure thing ma'am.
I'll be sure t'bring Bruno along wit me."
I winked at her
while I nodded at Johnny Boy
who once again point'd at me t'move from his sight.

That night in the prison yard

right after supper
Bruno'n I smoked our evenin' cigarettes.

the picnic table Bruno sat on bowed an' bent
as he rested his arms
'long the cracks'n crevices a'the boards.
wit his cigarette pinch'd b'tween his finger n'thumb
he brought it t'his lips an' made the tip bleed ash
as the orange faded t'black jus' like the night at hand.

"Arlene was lookin' fer ya today,"
I said with a heavy exhale of smoke.

"what did the pretty lady want wit me?"

"what th'fuck do I know of her business?
besides the fact that Johnny Boy went'n told her
I were you and she believed him."

"dumb broad."

"well she wants t'see us next week…"
I continued.

"what a waste'a time.
we ain't got any sob stories t'tell her,"
he insisted standin' up from the table.

"maybe we do,"
I implied.

Bruno's face contorted
"what you gettin' on 'bout?"

"she might be our ticket
outta this joint,"
I roused.

After my proclamation

Bruno'n I headed back t'our cell
wit our arms loaded with the day's profits.
cigarettes that'd last months b'tween the two'a us
and an idea that'd soon come t'fruition.

just ahead of us stood an informant of mine—
the kinda guy ya keep close
'cause he had more answers than questions
an' more importantly
mouths outside the walls
that granted me the information I needed.
I nodded t'Bruno that I'd catch up wit him shortly
an' veered over t'the man leaning 'gainst the brick wall
wit his foot bent
lookin' like he were holdin' the structure up.

I reached out my hand
an' in exchange he placed an envelope
with'a wax seal on the back
that was red as'a rose
with a "T" in the center.
we nodded with the trade
as I retrieved a carton of cigs from my armpit
an' placed 'em in his outstretch'd hand.

I turned to walk away
an' like deja vu was'a man who walked in my direction
who was identical t'the man I just made an exchange wit.
he gave me a look'a satisfaction
while he brushed past me seein'
my fulfilled arms and hand.

I glanced ov'r my shoulder
t'see identical twin brothers
lightly shakin' hands
whisperin' secrets into each other's ears
with'a posture of satisfaction.

I caught up to Bruno

who'd already been givin' stares
at the butt hurt boys who'd lost a lot that day.
he noticed the missin' carton a'cigs from under my arm

"lookin' a box short
hope they gone'n got you what ya needed."

assuredly I spoke up
"them boys never let me down."

Once we got to our cell

we dropped our spoils on the bed
an' proceeded t'count the tobacco.
there were enough cigs t'cover the floor a'the cell
an' then some.
Bruno picked one up
began twirlin' it under his nose
as he inhaled deeply
the sweetest smell in all the world he claimed.

his inhale was as deep as the ocean
while the scent trails touched ev'ry hair'n his nostrils
ticklin' the senses
arousin' his olfactory recall t'his first ever cigarette.

That first taste of nicotine on his tongue

was like nectar from the sweetest flower—
the kind even bees dream of tastin'.

it was a victory cig
the kind ya smoke with satisfaction
pulsin' through yer veins
where the world around ya is dark
like that of'a midnight sky
an' the only light is that ember on the tip
burnin' hot like the sun
meltin' them emotions of regret
an' sadness
…an' madness…

that sweet smell'a victory
wasn't just the carbon monoxide
bein' pushed outta his lungs
no…
it were that smell of freshly poured
gasoline…
an' cedar…
an' flesh…
from the bodies he caught fire
wit the fire in his heart.

The memory was interrupted

as a mouse-like voice echoed
through our tiny cell of brick'n mortar
"I don't think I caught your name
in our passing earlier...
you are?"
Arlene asked politely.

in'a prison full'a men
all with diff'rent backgrounds'n history
ain't none'a them had what I had
when it came to a name
an' it wasn't fear I was tryin' t'instill
rather, the first lather of deceit
in what I hoped would be my way outta that prison.

I stated
"my name's Michael."

RYAN A. KOVACS

THE CHESS PIECES

If the men a part of my plan

were set up like chess pieces
the board would be filled with'a bunch'a pawns.
'bout everyone of 'em were expendable
could only move forward one step at'a time
an' merely served as a blockade
or the means of gettin' in the way'a those who'd try'n stop me.
however, the valuable pieces start'd wit my knights—
the twins.

they were my informational portal
t'the outside world
where they had people workin' fer them
gatherin' information 'bout my father's whereabouts.

while on the outside, I'd been trackin'm down
but his trail went'n gone cold when I got lock'd up
and it wasn't 'til I met those unique brothers
that I found all hope was not lost.
like the knights'n chess
they are calculated maneuverer's
and nev'r trace their steps.
a modern day ninja you'd likely call 'em
'cause they were silent'n deadly
t'wards anyone that dared cross 'em.

Pete and re-Pete

grew up
with nothin' in their lives bein' diff'rent.

they were quite literally
the exact same person through'n through.

no one could tell 'em apart
nor knew the other one's name.

Pete was the older one
an' re-Pete was the young'r one
or the other way 'round.
not a single person seemed t'know
let alone validate the claim.

no one could ever tell if they's were tellin'
the truth
'cuz one'd lie and the other'd swear to it
an' only one of 'em would admit to bein'
a traitor.
jus' never knew which one...

That's what got them locked up

betrayin' the muth'fuckin' government.

the story ain't straight here but
when I tell ya one faked his death t'cover fer the other
that much is true.
they were spooks train'd in espionage
by the CIA or NSA or some shit.
an' while one would receive trainin'
he'd come home'n train the brother
an' switch it up on the daily
without anyone ever knowin'
creatin' not one, but two perfect spies.

Shortly after their initiation
one was sent over as'a spy t'the Soviet Union
to help aid the U.S. government
durin' the early years of the Cold War.
the two paired up
completin' missions on the double
turnin' in him'n her
killin' few
an' torturing many.
they played more games than
them damned reindeer in that silly song
my mother'd sing t'me when I were young.

Believe it or not

they made more friends than enemies
'cause they started recruitin' t'start their own war.

while over'n the Soviet Union they found the collapse
a'two great nations was 'bout as easy
as'a two time hooker lookin' t'score some extra cash.

once they went in t'radio silence on both sides
a major effort went into finding the only one
they gone thought existed.

The story goes

the Soviets gone'n black bagged Pete
and the U.S. gone'n swiped up re-Pete
in a mission they hoped would end the war.
confused, the U.S. government used re-Pete
as'a disguise t'obtain the traitor the Soviets captured.
little'd both sides know
that the two were in fact brothers
an' at a special meetin' site in Butugychag
the brothers were able t'take down
the secret agents who'd reunited 'em back together.

however, Pete had been severely tortured by the Soviets
a madman named Kazimir Stepanov
tainted the brother's appearance by carvin'
his nation's flag on Pete's forehead.
in order t'keep their followers
foreign'n domestic
they needed t'uphold the sacred bond'a brotherhood
an' thus Pete went'n tortured his own 'brat' as they say
by retracin' the same design on re-Pete.

No matter what

their background was
they's were the most reliable
sum'bitches this place had t'offer.

their delivery t'me the previous day
was the possible profile picture of a man
taken ov'r a hun'red feet away
wit more granules than a sandbox
that they believed t'be my father.

I studied the picture well
seein' that salt'n pepper hair
an' half a mustache I remember
he'd often stroke with anticipation.

there were no discernible way t'tell
if that picture were really the man
I was riskin' so much t'break outta there for
but somethin' in my heart
whatever was left of it
after that day in my closet
told me it were him.

however, there'd only be one
tell-tale sign a'his existence.

ya see my father used t'be an alcoholic
but nev'r at his own hands.
his philosophy b'hind it were
if someone'd offer him'a drink
he could never turn it down
yet never drank of his own free will.
when a friend or family member'd come ov'r the house
or father'd go out t'the local bar
there'd be nights he'd play wit fire
pokin' temptation like a kid wit'a stick
waitin' fer someone to offer'm up a drink

and then he'd toast
his notorious Latin line

"non mea culpa hoc potu sum."

"Not my fault that I am drinking"

was his tell
before he'd turn in t'the man I grew t'know.

my father
 the beat'r
  the gambl'r
   the drink'r
    the sinn'r
     the undertak'r
     the kill'r
      the deceiv'r

the man
who was only livin' fer one purpose

t'die by my hands.

My father

fought in the second world war
an' saw more things decent
than decrepit.
he was part'a the clean up crew
never seein' a lick'a action
nor firin' his rifle.
by the time he stepped foot
on foreign soil
the war'd been over for'a week
an' he was a weaker man for it.

all the celebratory booze he'd consumed
was 'nough t'supply the 442nd infantry regiment
'til he came home n'swore
he'd never consume a drink
of his own free will again.

But little did he know

his addiction
gone'n got the best of him
an' his sorry excuse of an existence
when he gone'n met my mother in…

you fuckin' guessed it

a bar.

Of course

it were after the war
an' he wooed her in wit his stories
the ones he often told
that were stricken wit fear an' disgust
but mos'of all, sorrow
in the way he described the bodies
laid 'cross the roads'n ditches.

from my experience
the ones that lived through it
an' witnessed the carnage
never spoke of it
an' if they did
it was one time fer validation—
twice if it were a lie.

Problem is

most people that tell a good story
don't have'a problem tellin' it.

it's the hard stories people tell
that give 'em away.

The king is the enemy

in'a game of chess.
he's the one yer tryin' t'get to
the one you strategically
maneuver pieces on the board
past his defensive wall
where he puts others at risk
in order t'protect himself
all while ya sacrifice yer own pieces
attemptin' t'get to him
constantly puttin' him in check
where he'll shimmy outta the way
makin' one move away
tryin' to distract you from
the corner you'll soon put him in
'til ya get'm there
right where ya want him
upon exclaiming to him

check mate.

But you don't get there alone.

no.

you can't.

you have an army at yer disposal
one that'll get ya there t'that corner
where that sad king'll stand
afraid and defenseless
'bout t'lose the war he gone'n started.

you'll sacrifice the crooked rooks
b'cause they only move
side t'side
up'n down
followin' orders without any question
in hopes they'll be part'a the slaughter.

an' the bishops don't go straight
they're all over the place
yet serve the purpose'a sniping from afar.
they'll get their time in the light
b'fore they're spotted an' taken out
one by one.

The queen however

is the sneakiest of 'em all
able t'move anywhere on the board
who is considered t'be the most valuable piece
as she cuts corners like a saw
surroundin' herself wit those she knows will follow
'til she slays pieces
that'r trapped on the squares
they are bound to
pickin'em off
one atta-time 'til she allows the final strike.

my dearest Arlene
likely hadn't known the plan had been
set'n motion wit her small pass
an' gentle gaze
but she were the queen'a the game
we were 'bout t'play
as we struck first with
pawn to king 4
against my father
8 blocks away.

BEHAVIOR

The day that replays

over'n over in my head
ain't no time worth retracin'
not worth measurin'
lest rememberin'

but I do.

there are details 'bout it that
don't make no sense
an' ev'rytime I try's t'remember
my mind goes dark
like a switch turned from on t'off.

memory is like the rain:

sometimes it's soft, drizzlin' lightly
like yer bein' stroked with a soft feather
that's impossible t'hear and nev'r truly wetting
yet, kindly letting ya know it's there.
   those memories are gentle
   fading glimpses'a joy n'love—
      a time not present.

other times it's fallin', plummeting heavily
like yer bein' pelted by rocks
while clouds overhead create roars'a rollin' thunder
as ya drown amidst the water that drops.
   those memories are heavy
   omnipresent chunks'a disbelief—
      a time that is my present.

There she was

my mother
wrapped in'a yellow'n brown stained apron
wearin' it like it were a part a'her skin.
it draped 'round her waist like a necklace would
with'a 'nough slack t'show her workin' hands
had a place to always dry themselves.

often when she used the knife
after she gone'n cut up fresh fruit'n vegetables
she'd place the knife b'tween her apron
"blade t'the sky,"
she'd say
an' pinch it as she slid it through'r finger tips
dryin' the metal
leavin' a thin haze of juice along the edge.

she knew how t'use a knife
for more than jus' slicin'n dicin'
after she'd cut the head off'a chicken fer dinner.
I could see the smallest bit'a remorse
whenever she'd do the deed
as if the animal were somehow sacred
but father'd always exclaim
"we ain't at the top a'the food chain t'eat grass."

Father was always cold hearted

rarely showin' any signs of affection
or love.
his prefer'd method a'love was
tough love
an' he had a certain way of showin' it
of'en wit his fists.

normally he pummeled me with
angry love   or
drunk love   or
forgotten love   or
weak love   or
straight up love of hittin'   me.

His love

was bludgeoning
was overpowering
was elating
was controlling
an' he loved his own love
more than he loved mother'n I.
it were love like no other
where it'd

cackle
  and
POP!

you right in the fuckin' nose.

It was love nonetheless

mother would declare
after a night'a fightin' him off her.
this was the man she'd married
an' there were no way outta marriage
"accept through death,"
she confided in me one night.

it was there that an idea grew
one that blossom'd through the winter
in t'that hot summer day
where ghosts danced'n swayed 'round my mind
like a curtain flailin' in the wind.

it's a day that weighs heavy as an anvil
while it crushes me day in an' day out.

but this was the story I had t'tell
an' there wit Arlene
is where the plan got set'n motion.

"Good morning,"

Arlene's voice was fearless
as I sat b'fore her
while she proceeded t'open her white notebook.
I sat 'cross from'r as she gently crossed
her milky white legs.
they looked soft'n smooth
like she'd bathed in canola oil
while my mouth watered
imagin'n what they'd taste like.

but I'd learnt my lesson from
the dumb sons'a bitches b'fore me
who'd gone in there t'talk
hopin' for some kinda exchange
in dialogue and clothes
an' bodily fluids.
I weren't there for such petty things
I had'a goal
I had'a mission
an' if I lured the right prey
wit my encin' scent of musk'n charm
I wouldn't be feared fer the predator I was.

I wasn't quite sure

how the conversation should start
after the greetin'
while I just stared at Arlene
jus' waitin' for her t'say something more.

"is your friend Bruno coming?"
she pressed.

"he don't do well wit closed in spaces,"
I nudged.

"that's odd.
well, what about you
do you do good in closed in spaces?"

feelin' a bit perturbed at
the rate the conversation had been going
I muster'd
"I do just fine."

Arlene click'd her pen
that sound'd like a tick on'a clock
as she jotted down a few scribbles in'r notebook.

"whatcha writin'?"
I inquired.

"findings,"
she muttered.

"what ya find?"
I pestered.

"just a few things.
nothing to worry about, Sugar."

Sugar?

was I some kinda additive
t'her concoction of criminals?
was this an invitation of hers
to allow me t'mix wit her like that of coffee
where I'd dissolve in t'the taste
of beans'n water?
was this her perception a'me
thinkin' I were sweet talkin' t'her
expecting a knee slappin' one liner?
was it a word she spoke t'all her clients
openin' a door for some sexual innuendo
where she'd then get her client t'confess
their true motives
an' then say her notorious line?

I hesitated

b'fore my boldness overtook
my look of hesitation.

"ya call all yer clients 'Sugar'?"

"no, just you,"
she winked while hiding
an intrepid smile.

I was a virgin

t'the openin' up
talkin'bout my feelings and junk.
gran'ed we didn't get in t'the juicy stuff
at that point
as our first meetin' was a bit informal
an' had more
unspoken tension
than
spoken words.

truth be told
I think I had'a better cover
wit my fake smile
than she
with her rich intentions.

Her mission was

-t'rehabilitate broken minds
-put people on'a path to success
-understand people
-ask tough questions
an' most importantly

-help people get outta prison.

Near the end

of our conversation
I had t'ask the obvious question

"how long these sessions usually last?"

"depends on the man,"
she insinuated.

"well ma'am, I've seen some
a'these men come in here
an' be tossed out like yesterday's trash.
jus' wonderin' what the expectation is."

"most men can't hold their load
of trash that spews from their mouths.
they don't come in here for help.
they come in here for release,"
she implied.
"once they've said their
meaningless garbage
which is usually sexually oriented
I dismiss them because I'm not here for favors.
I am here for results."

"plucky statement.
what makes ya think
I ain't here fer sexual favors?"
I questioned.

"because you are holding out for something.
what, I don't know exactly.
but you want to be here
and that intrigues me,"
she blushed.

"are ya sayin' you wanna help me?"
I pushed.

"however I am able to, Sugar,"
she gestured with'a slight bite of'r lip.

That's all I needed

an' her reassurance was assuring
at least for the moment.

I dismissed myself
exitin' her office with'a plan formulating
like clouds in'a hurricane.

I caught up wit Bruno who'd been eyein'
some'a the boys in the courtyard.
he had a distasteful look about him
one that rendered the question
"what has y'all burned up?"

"these piece of shit faggots
that's what."

"whoa nah!"
I chuckled lightly
"one of'em ask t'suck yer pecker?"

Bruno gave me the look of death
as he peered long in t'my eyes
"there's a rumor going on about us.
had ya not been sweet talkin' t'your
little piece'a ass
you'd heard the words that been floating
like farts in the wind."

the news was unbefitting
'specially after the fear we thought
we'd instill'd wit the benchin' bets.
men had been eatin' outta the palms
of our hands
only t'bite a fuckin' finger off
an' tellin' us to go fuck ourselves with it.

Trouble was going to be had

upon findin' the person responsible
fer starting the rumor statin'
Bruno sucks dick for three smokes
an' enjoys bein' peed on
after he's been fucked from b'hind.
according t'Bruno
he'd been asked a handful'a times that day
fer some action
while someone pissed on'm in the bathroom
b'cause they'd been raped in bet losses.

if I said the man was tick'd off
it'd be the understatement a'the year.

the man's blood boiled like lava
in an underwater fissure
while apparent steam shot from his head.

if y'all thought I were fixated
on the goal'a killin' my father
Bruno gone'n raised the ante.

It didn't take long

t'track down a lead from good'ol Pete'n re-Pete
an' two packs of cigs
the very next day
jus' t'get a name…

Dallas

the mother fuckin'
dick suckin'
butt fuckin'
swallows everything that comes in contact wit his mouth
son-of-a-bitch
who lost the most on the bet 'gainst Bruno
gone'n dug his own grave.

ya see
there were'a group of them boys
that thought themselves t'be sailors
stickin' it in dirty holes of other men
'cause fancy Arlene denied 'em the glory hole
an' rosy palm with her five sisters just weren't enough
t'get the job done apparently.

them boys were easy t'spot.
after all
Dallas was the one t'thank
fer the permanent reminder
they each wore on their faces.
little red bumps that spread like
butter on bread
fittin' in t'the nooks'n crannies
in the corners of their mouths.

If you guessed

that the moment of confrontation
was 'bout as epic as'a greek mythological battle
where odds were not stacked in any favor a'the protagonist
you'd be more right
than the right hook Bruno caught
upon enterin' the dinin' facility
where them dick lickers were waitin'
t'get a big'ol piece of the man
that raped 'em more in winnings
than they did newcomers.

The rupturing sound

of Daniel's fist connectin' wit Bruno's jaw
was like hearin'a two by four snap ov'r a concrete block.

Bruno barely even flinched
'til his eyes made direct contact with Daniel's face
an' wit no hesitation
pivoted his feet
turnin' hard in t'his undercut swing
sending Daniel sailin' t'wards the dinning table.

upon his landing
which was that of hearin' a butcher
slam a slab'a meat on a choppin' block
Bruno gone'n glared at the remaining nine men
who thought they'd had a childish prayer
of takin' down
the behemoth Bruno turn'd in to.

Within seconds

Bruno'd cleared close to twenty yards
headin' in the direction of his newly acquainted enemies
as they all braced themselves
fer what would later be described as
the extermination of Dallas an' company
because the only thing bein' spread
other than the bubbly affliction in the corners'a their mouths
was the blood spewed from ev'ry orifice of their bodies.

Between me and a few others

the number'a witnesses t'confess what they'd seen
was hardly worth the free admission t'the bloodbath that ensued
yet instilled a certain kinda fear
that could likely be consider'd terrifying
like that of a man treadin' water
watchin' a dorsal fin emerge
while darting in his direction.

If you can imagine

how a shark strikes in its natural habitat
glidin' through the water
like moving fingers ov'r silk b'tween yer fingertips
you'd likely understand how Bruno moved
past his surroundings
while maintainin' speed'n accuracy
as he
snapp'd fingers
  broke ribs
ripp'd clothing
  cut skin
smash'd noses
  tore muscles
fractur'd vertebrae
all while heavin' bodies like bags'a flour
carrying
dragging
pulling
an'
flailing
men in each direction 'til he reached
the cowboy himself.

Dallas came prepared

thrustin' a shiv in t'Bruno's peck
but not in time for Bruno t'grab'm by the balls
where he squeezed as tight as'a boa constrictor
rupturin' the guy's nads.

before Dallas could pass out from the pain'n shock
Bruno grabbed him by the back of the skull
a famous grip Dallas likely knew all to well
'cept he was 'bout to be on the receivin' end
of the one thing that would make'm spit
as Bruno violently plowed his face in t'the concrete wall
jerkin' Dallas's face
poundin' it like a war drum
'til the sounds of thudding
became sticky and moist wit the amount'a blood
leaking from his face.

CONSEQUENCES

Thirty days in the black box

is what they gone'n gave Bruno fer his outburst
an' it wasn't even for his attack on ten men
that stood 'bout as much'a chance at survival
than that of 'a fly caught in a spider's web.

nah, he got the box for hittin' that big bitch
Johnny Boy
when he were attempting t'pry Bruno off Dallas'
disfigured body.

of course yours truly here
ran to aid the man who didn't need no help
but dammit if there were an opportunity t'get my paws
on Johnny Boy
you can b'sure I were gonna take advantage of that.

But my plan was futile

as my stealthy strategy would not
come to fruition while security guards
stormed the dinnin' hall catching me
inchin' behind Johnny
like a lion ready t'pounce on its prey.

within moments after the initial attack
all I felt were'a crack b'hind my head
an' all went black fer awhile.

The worst way to wake up

is water bein' splashed in yer face
I gots to admit.
gran'ed I ain't never been woken up worse b'fore
than that day in my room
when I were jus' seven years old.

my mother frantically slammin' my bedroom door
flippin' the light switch on
where it blinded my black vision
b'hind my eyelids.

I awoke to her words.

words   that penetrated my ears
seepin' deep like a pit'a quick sand.
words   that captur'd fear
grabbin' me like a handshake wit'a stranger.
words   that permanently fasten'd
lockin' in place like a seatbelt.

words

that I would
never
hear
again.

But there I was

water rollin' down my cheek
mixin' wit blood'n sweat
an' the confusion of where I was.

Johnny's voice throbbed 'round my head
like that of'a thumb after smashin' it wit a hammer.

"you gone'n fucked up pal,"
he said wit'a smirk on his face.
"yer little stunt in the dinning hall there
gonna cost you some hard time in the box."

"is it now?"
I asked sarcastically.

"there wasn't a good reason t'do
what ya did to them men
regardless of the entertainment value.
but, what you were gonna do t'me
well, that's a damn sin."
his hand gripped the baton
tightly b'fore he wound up
an' swung a home run
square 'cross my face.

grabbin' my chin he peered in t'me
like he were lookin' in the mirror
examining his own perplexed look
wit frustration, yet elation
"I know you're prolly enjoyin' this
but let me introduce ya to somethin' you won't."

as he nodded t'the guards restrainin' me
to take me to the black box
I went an' gave him one last stare
that issued'a warning, statin'
'you're gonna regret that…'

Let me tell you

Johnny regretted it
but not yet.

we aren't t'that part'a the story yet
but let me assure ya
I keep my promises.

don't ya forget that now.

Have you ever closed your eyes

an' embraced the blackness—
a void so endless an' obscure
that the vast wonder of what was conceived
was within sight?

now imagine that
with yer eyes open.

that's all I could see
lock'd in that damn black box.
shadows that turned t'puffs a'smoke
disapperin' like they weren't even there
when even I knew my hand was right'n'front a'me.

sometimes we get lost in ar'selves
thinkin' we know much 'bout us
that no one else does.
it's when we're alone that we retell secrets
whisperin' them t'ghosts we hope are listening
while we
reminisce 'bout the past
contemplate the future
an' second guess our present
all while maintainin' a simple thought process
that ask complex questions
yet, give convoluted answers.

But where was my mind

on the eve of my destructive revolution
when the plans I had
had been thwarted
givin' me less'n less
of'a chance t'do what I'd swore to do?

There was a knock on the door

an' behind it
a mouse-like voice
that muttered words like whispers
yet echoed demands.

lookin' around
tryin' t'find the exit wit my hands
sliding them 'cross concrete an' rock
like a blind person tryin' t'hone in
on the only senses he got left
I caught a faint scent
of cherry blossom perfume
seepin' its way through
the imperfect cracks in the walls and ceiling.

Arlene?

Her demands were authoritative

as she stomped her heel in t'the floor b'neath her.
nothin' was clickin' until I heard the lock on the door
unlatch from its hinge
an' light blinded me as if bein' born in t'this world again.

protectin' my eyes from the glare
I stood there fer a moment gatherin' myself
with uncertainty b'fore me.

finally her words began to jingle in my ears
"let's go, Sugar
our hour starts now
and it's a five minute walk to my office."

the guard gone'n stood there fer a moment
salivatin' ov'r Arlene's peach shaped bottom
forgettin' all 'bout me
as they escorted me t'her office.

Shutting the door behind her

as we both walked in
Arlene let out a sigh
like a paper bag bein' crushed.

you could sense she were stressed
from what I hadn't known
'til I gone'n asked her
through her flusterin' frustration
"what's got yer panties in a knot?"

she grinned wit hesitation
"these guards are less cooperative
than the damn inmates sometimes
I tell ya."

"oh, I thought you'd learnt that by now,"
I stated coyly.

she gave me'a look that shouted distaste
yet, she held back'a snicker that shouted relief.

"so what ya got me in here for?"
I asked with'a pressing tone.

"our weekly session of course!"
she stated excitedly.

Half way through

clearin' up rumors
an' given out reasons
them pansy boys deserved
ev'ry lick they took from Bruno
Arlene asked me point blank
"what do you want?"

"I'm afraid you'll have t'be more specific,"
I voiced.

"you come across as a man
who knows what he wants
and yet you've never disclosed that information to me.
so I'm curious
what exactly do you want?"
she pressed.

I don't think she was ready for the answer

so I sugarcoated my intent
"I wanna get outta here
this place
it's rotten an' reeks of sloth."

"sloth you say?
you continue to astonish me, Michael.
your vocabulary and insight
don't necessarily radiate from your stature.
may I ask how you became so educated?"

"yer sayin' I look dumb, ya?"
I asked angrily.

"no, no, Sugar
I meant no offense.
it's just that..."
she hesitated fer a moment
"it's just that
I've read your file
and while most of it is
in my professional opinion
a real tragedy
there's no documentation on your education
and barely anything about you before your record started
when you were a teenager,"
she noted.

"My mother told me once

that books are the doors to a writer's soul.
ya see
knowledge is learnt from studyin' words
while wisdom is obtained from studyin' people.
it's all 'bout how one applies the two t'gether
t'find the answer in their own life."

Arlene squinted t'wards me
"so then what's the answer for you?"

"to kill my mother-fuckin' father."

Taken aback

I could see Arlene display'r first ounce'a fear t'wards me
an' her uncomfortableness shed off her
like skin from a snake.
she became all too easy t'read
an' see past while she resisted
the flood'a overwhelmin' emotion
by writin' notes in'r notebook.

"what's the matter?
didn't like my answer much?"
I asked violently
standin' t'stretch from my chair.

without a flinch however
her demeanor remained calm
as she collect'd her thoughts in t'words
"we will have to explore the reasons
for these maddening thoughts you have.
but patricide is a new one for me."

Upon my exit

Arlene reached out t'grab my arm
pullin' me close'nough to smell her breath as she exhaled
"I'll see you in a week, Sugar.
don't think you've scared me off now."

b'fore she released her grip
her fingers slid down my forearm
feelin' like lightnin' on my skin—
shocking
burning
electrifying.

she winked nonchalantly
while I grinn'd as she called out
"guard, we are done here."

b'fore I could put thoughts t'words however
I sniffed once more
gatherin' her scent
that would swim in my nostrils
long in t'the days that came
while inside the black box
before the guard gone'n nudged my backside t'get movin'.

Towards the end of the hall

standin' jus' outside my lovely black room of'a cell
stood you know who—
Johnny Boy.

whackin' his baton in the palm of his hand
like he were ready t'put on a whoopin'.
he leaned in nice'n close t'my ear
makin' it a point t'tell me
"I know ya think Arlene
got them wet panties fer ya
but don't think yer conjugational visits of banter
aren't gonna cost ya
for the duration'a the time yer in here."

"sounds t'me like someone's jealous,"
I wise cracked.

"ain't no one here gonna save ya this time
you piece of shit,"
was the last thing I heard b'fore being slugged
'long the side'a the head
blackin' out once again.

RYAN A. KOVACS

INTERRUPTION

Stuck in the box

gave me a lot of time t'ponder what I'd divulge
to Arlene at each remainin' visit.
I didn't know much 'bout science
but chemistry was basic knowledge
in'a time of atom bombs an' nuclear power
so you'll have t'trust me when I tell ya
we were like a chemistry lab
mixin' and combustin'
creatin' reactions
that hadn't yet been discovered.

I never thought of myself as'a flirtatious fella
but Arlene claimed I had charm
an' that underneath this outside man
was pure innocence an' adoration

b'cause that's what I damn show'd her.

People are easy to deceive

because when ya give'm what they want
they typically choose not t'see the bullshit anymore
even when it's sittin' on their plate
right in front of 'em.

all you gotta do is convince them enough times
that the bullshit is the truth
an' spoon feed 'em 'til they think it tastes good.

because let's be honest
the truth never goes down easy.

And the truth was this:

I were usin' Arlene.
part'a me was convinced she hadn't a damn clue
yet, another part'a me wondered
if she were feedin' in t'me.

the basic rule of psychology is
not to feed into a patient's delusions.

but my words were far from delusional
hell, they weren't even threats
they were promises
vows even
an' I couldn't reiterate the point enough
that nothin' was gonna stop me from
killin' my father.

somehow
someway
I managed t'wrangle Arlene though
lassoing her like some enraged bull
'cept I was the bull
I just had'r convinced otherwise
an' no matter which way I went
she seemed t'follow me deeper down the rabbit hole.

Of course

that month in the black box
came'n went
an' my weekly headache
from head-bashin' Johnny
after each visit wit Arlene
was gettin' old quick.

my last day in there I got out early
fer my monthly physical.

law says I got a right to stay healthy in prison
yet, when I complained t'the doc
'bout my concussion symptom of'a headache
he gone'n told me they don't prescribe meds
for self-inflicted wounds.

"the fuck you mean self-inflicted?"
I asked infuriated.

"report here says
while in your cell, you repeatedly banged your head
against the concrete walls in order to get out once a week
for... therapy appointments,"
the doc quoted.

"who wrote that?"

"I'm afraid I can't disclose that information to you
inmate,"
the doc exclaimed coldly.

Hopping off the table

I snuck up b'hind him
grabbed the back'a his neck
thrustin' him down on his desk
while papers shifted an' glided t'the floor.

holdin' him down
pinching the nerves on the side'a his neck
I leaned ov'r to snag the report from his tremblin' hand.

tryin' t'talk I forced him further in t'his desk
applyin' pressure wit my finger an' thumb
that made his body limp
as I glanced at the file.

you can guess who forged the report
an' signed nicely on the dotted line.

seems as though Johnny kept promises too.

fucker.

But there was more

after my discharge wit the prescription of
suck-it-the-fuck-up-buttercup
from the doc who looked like he had himself an
asphyxiation addiction with the marks I left on his neck
I arrived at my cell
t'find ev'rything in shambles.

mattresses cut open an' flat on the floor
toilet seat broken off an' in half
shelves barren wit the books that were on 'em
torn, cut and stripped of pages.

Bruno walked up b'hind me
"that's not the worst of it."

"the fuck you mean?"
I asked with pure rage.

Each and every one of our cigarettes

were broken in half like matchsticks
wit lines'a tobacco spellin' out on the floor
'you're mine asshole.'

Bruno clenched his fists

jus' as tight as mine
as we stared long'n hard at the chaos in our cell.

neither of us spoke much to each other
despite not havin' seen one another for a month
but when the silence was no longer needed
we both sat on the edge of our tatter'd beds
hunched ov'r staring emptily at the tile
contemplatin' our reuniting conversation.

"I'm gonna kill'm,"
Bruno muttered.

"no. we are gonna kill'm.
t'gether."

We bowed our heads once more

an' sank into our own thoughts
'bout murder'n hate'n flat out mayhem.

I imagine Bruno were envisionin' how
he wanted t'kill Johnny.
catching him all alone down some hallway
sneakin' up b'hind him
gettin' them big bear-like hands 'round his head
an' twisting quickly
severin' his neck from his spine
lookin' deep into his eyes
right b'fore they rolled t'the back of his skull
until his paralyzed body fell like a sack'a shit t'the floor.

unlike Bruno however
my mind traversed the unusual
and like poetry, I daydreamed of my favorite color
an' how well it'd look on Johnny's dead body.
but the simple fact remained
I would need to see all the colors the world had t'offer first
b'fore my favorite would bleed through.

It was Tuesday once again

an' Arlene was gettin' pushy.
pestering me wit questions
that weighed 'bout as heavy as'a sigh
but worthless with intent.

"how was your reunion with Bruno
after being apart for a month?
did you miss him?"
she asked politely
with'r hands folded on her lap.

when I looked up at her
it had occurred t'me it were the first time
I'd seen her face since our session began.

she was wearin' a new pair'a glasses
oval in shape wit thicker than usual frames.
it were as if they had magnified the size'a her eyeballs
as they peered into mine.
I felt the slightest bit controlled by her
like she were some archeologist chippin' away at me
findin' the outline an' brushin' off the excess nothingness.

"we ain't lovers. I hope you're not implyin' that,"
I answered.

"you're friends yeah? it's okay to miss your friend,"
she retorted.

"fine, yeah, sure, I missed him.
what diff'rence does it make?"

"well it seems odd that you both received the same punishment
yet, each of you committed different offenses.
why do you think that is?"

I was gettin' edgy

an' that whole patience thing was bein' tested
"because Johnny Boy got a hard on fer fuckin' wit us."

"did he do something to you, Sugar?"
she asked wholeheartedly.

"makes no difference what he did
only that he's gonna regret it."

surprised, Arlene inquired
"what can I do to help?"

My attitude changed

an' so did my elation when at that very moment
Pete burst through the door holdin' onto an envelope
wit the unbroken seal
yellin' to me
"I found him!"

Excusing myself from the room

Pete gone'n pulled me towards the nearest corner
t'whisper his thoughts.

"a buddy of mine happened to be out one night
about a week ago at some hole in the wall bar.
he got drinking with a guy he just met there
who wasn't drinking
and after some time talking
my buddy offered to buy him a drink."

I interrupted eagerly
"did he say it?
did he say the words?"

a voice crept up from b'hind me
as re-Pete continued the story
"no.
however, the two men got through talking the
usual drunk stories
woe is me kind of deal
towards the end of the night
and just before the bar was starting to close
an older gentleman walks up behind my buddy
and says to the bartender
he wants to close his tab.
the bartender jokingly says to the man
you're good tonight
like always.
then all of a sudden the drunk guy my buddy just met
speaks up and says for the three of them to do one last round
on him
and the older gentlemen starts speaking latin
when the bartender gives him his shot."

"the tell,"
I spoke thrillingly.

Pete continued
"the envelope has all the details.
oh, and a little welcome back gift for ya.
sorry it's late."
re-Pete pulled from under the backside'a his shirt
a full carton of cigs
placin' them an' the envelope in my hands
while the two of 'em walked off in diff'rent directions.

Frantically I opened the sealed envelope

like some excited kid at Christmas
who knew what he were openin'.

A note was inside that read:

Enclosed is the address to where
your presumed father resides.
Take caution from here on out
and don't let your need blind your actions.
Time is not an enemy but a friend
with patience.

p.s. No repayment on cigs.
We bet against you on the bench.

-Traitors

My hands trembled

at the sheer thought of known'
the information that would lead me t'my father.

b'hind the brothers' note was the key
that would unlock potential
an' drive me t'the edge of confrontation
to the man I vowed to kill
b'cause of what he took from me
an' what he made me do.
like'a dog beggin' for a table scrap
I started t'drool
wit saliva poolin' in the back'a'my throat
wetting my appetite fer blood'n revenge.

I went t'turn the page
when suddenly the note was ripped from my grasp.
focused only on the letter
I had let my guard down an' had tunnel vision
nev'r noticin' Johnny Boy creepin' up the side'a me
stealin' away the chance fer my eyes
t'memorize the pen strokes on the paper
that divulged the details of the present
whereabouts of my father
which stemmed back t'the past where it all started.

"oh, what's this we got'ere?
a love note from the Peter twins.
looks like someone likes a little ménage à trois action?"
Johnny posed.

his attempt at French was insulting
an' sounded like someone talkin' in English wit their mouth full.
I was far from entertained
and demanded my letter back
"now that you've had your unamusin' one-liner
how's 'bout you give me that letter back?"

"would that get me in your good graces?
would that make you like me?"
his tone was whiny and sarcastic.

"it would decrease the amount'a time
it takes t'kill you,"
I declared.

"you hear that boys
that sounded like a threat.
but rather than beat you weekly
an' have to walk down the hall t'pull you outta your cell
we can make the punishment
drag out 'round here."

b'hind me, three guards stepped within arms length
each wit their batons drawn'n ready.

"boys, yer about to witness an inmate have an accident.
do add in your report the inmate struck me
after I tried t'help him which resulted in his broken fingers,"
Johnny exclaimed excitedly.

He raised his baton high in the air

an' swung down swiftly
with momentum that of'a pendulum.

much t'his surprise however
I went'n caught it before strikin' my face.
his eyes popped like'a kernel of corn
as I stepped under his arm
twistin' the baton out from his fingers
then knockin' him 'cross the back'a his head
showin' him the same treatment he gone'n showed me.

"there, now your report isn't a full fuckin' lie."

"YOU ASSHOLE!
you will regret that more than ya know!
get 'em!"
Johnny shouted.

A man has to recognize

when he's been beat
even b'fore the fight's begun.

I went'n took the brothers' advice
recognizin' that this fight was but a scrimmage
in the all out war that'd be happenin' on 'em.

t'understand the complexity'a the situation
it became abundantly clear t'me
if a few broken fingers were all I had t'suffer
then so be it.

When the men held me down

I wrestled like a mule
kickin' my legs like a slingshot
rollin' like a pig in mud
snarlin' like a gator in shallow water.

I didn't make it easy fer 'em to hold my arm down
my dominant hand too of course
while Johnny came down on my index an' middle fingers
like that of'a sledgehammer.

the breaking sound was like the crack of'a whip
as my fingers curled an' swelled upon impact.
I didn't give'm the satisfaction of a whimper
or scream
but rather asked simply "are ya done?"

his smirk was devilish
like he'd grown horns an'a tail
wit fire all around'm.

"yeah, sure.
but one more thing..."

You can go on and guess

what that one more thing was.

a nice
fat
throbbing
pounding
pulsating

headache.

PICKING UP PIECES

I had a dream

that I was walkin' up to a large white house
wit dark blue shudders faded from the sun
an' paint chipp'd from dry heat.

a narrow clothesline hung clean clothes—
aprons'n jean overalls with stains on 'em
flappin' in the gentle gusts of wind.

beyond the green yard laid barren fields
dried up an' thirsty fer rain t'grow the crops beneath.

I approached the front porch
steppin' up each creaking step that bowed
until I reached the front door
an' entered.

silk-like curtains danced in the windowsill
like a pair'a ghosts doin' a waltz t'the sound'a silence.

walking in t'the kitchen
I could smell'a fresh baked pecan pie.
as I lifted the checker'd cloth from upon it
a loud thud hit the floorboards upstairs.

sneakily investigating the noise
I crept upstairs to find a door down the hall half opened.
as I began t'approach the door
I noticed a still hand lying on the floor.
when I moved in clos'r
I pushed the door open t'find
a body sprawled out and lifeless—

Arlene.

No sooner did I recognize her

did I hear'a faint noise from b'hind me.
I turned 'round an' much t'my surprise
stood a short, sheeted figure holdin' a bloody knife.

b'fore I could muster a word
the figure screamed incoherently
chargin' at me wit the knife.

unable t'react
the blade gone'n pierced my side
sendin'a sharp pain throughout my body.

I awoke to feel

shooting pain radiatin' up my arms from my fingertips.
Johnny apparently kept good on his promise
breakin' two'a my fingers on one hand
an' my thumb on the other.

the cast the doc put on my hand
with the broken index and middle fingers
looked like I had'a gun fer an extremity
an' the other hand was givin'a persistent thumbs up.

Bruno looked on at me

"they gone'n fucked ya up good.
sorry I weren't there t'help."

his sympathy was genuine
but he knew as much as me
this was jus' the beginnin'.

"I managed t'snag the carton of cigs from the brothers,"
he added.

"where's the letter?"
I questioned.

"well, 'bout that…"
Bruno was cut off abruptly

"that letter you be lookin' for
I gots it right here,"
Johnny gawked from outside our cell.
"I'll tell ya what
I'm a nice guy despite what ya might think
and I'll make you a deal.
I'll give you a piece'a this letter each day
fer'a month as long as you're on yer best behavior.
ya do what I say
when I say it
with no questions asked
an' by the time the month ends
you'll have all the precious pieces'a the letter
you seem t'be more attached to than yer dick,"
Johnny exclaimed.

I was at his mercy

an' remembered what the brothers wrote in their note
'don't let my need blind my actions'.

I nodded with contempt
but seethed at the mouth
as it were but jus' another test of my
patience.

Johnny began to rip the letter

into pieces and fragments
torturin' my eyes into belief
of the destruction he were creatin' b'fore me.

he went'n entered our cell
proceedin' t'the toilet
wit guards drawn an' ready t'pounce
had we met'm with trouble
reached into his palm pullin' out a random piece
an' dropped it in the water
where he then unzipped his pants
an' began t'piss on the shredded paper.
jus' b'fore finishing though
he went'n shook the remainin' drops
on t'Bruno's boots claimin'
"I know ya like t'get piss'd on
after you've been fucked."

like an addict I dropped t'the floor
shovin' my hand in t'the yellow colored water
hopin' to save the ink on the paper from smearin'
but to my dismay
havin' my thumb stickin' straight up
an' my other two fingers straight out
the ability to pinch was out of reach.

Johnny cackled at the sight
"sucks to suck
you piece of shit!"

his exit was relieving
yet, made me fume
like'a tanker truck that caught fire.

Bruno reached down b'tween my arms
into the piss water
placin' the soggy piece of paper in his bear like palm

studyin' it
"it's a start."

"what's it say?"

"it's a line.
could be 'bout any letter in the alphabet."

shit.

The process was long

an' dragged out like a heavy sigh.
the images of torture that grew in my mind
were as barbaric as
drawin' and quarterin'
or
tyin' Johnny's body to a horse
that'd pull'm for miles without end
or
straight up just rippin' him in half
like'a piece'a paper
by pullin' him from both ends of his body.

I expressed my disgruntled opinion

wit Arlene in our next session
where she were empathetic t'my situation.

I explained ev'rything t'her in great detail
an' apologized fer my quick exit from our last session.

"so, I have t'ask ya
b'fore I left last, you asked
how you could help me.
what exactly did ya mean?"
I inquired.

"truth is, Michael
there's just something about you
that has me flustered.
every time I think I know something
you go and make me question it.
I want to know you.
I want to help you.
but a gal has needs too you know,"
she declared with the bitin' of 'r lower lip.

"jus' what kinda needs?"

"I need to know what happened
to your mother and father."

"that's not'a need, Doll
that's a want,"
I retorted.

"that's not true.
I need to know because
of what I'm willing to sacrifice for you
and whether it's worth it."

"trust me when I tell ya then

it's worth it.
jus' don't give me yer sympathy
'cause that shit don't matter no more,"
I agreed.
In the back of my mind

I didn't quite know if she were ready
t'hear my story
nor do I think you are ready either
'cause this tale don't have no happy endin'.

only justification.

Whatever was justified to me however

needed t'be convincing to Arlene
an' it was imperative to allow her
to draw her own conclusions
just as you do
'bout a man such as me
who seeks more than jus' revenge.

how do I persuade her?
how do I persuade you?
into understandin' my reckoning
so that everybody
knows'n feels my satisfaction?

I ain't a man that sugarcoats the truth.
I ain't a man that is brutal wit it either.
but this is my story
an' it'll end the way I intend.

Johnny had lots of favors to ask

in which case I were damned
like'a hound from hell t'obey.
he dangled that letter b'fore my face
fer two whole weeks
givin' me shreds here'n there
that added up t'nothin' more
than indistinct lines or curves t'letters
which couldn't have ever been solved
even by Sherlock Holmes himself.

but one day after a brief encounter wit Arlene
who'd come in for some things from'r office
Johnny caught himself an idea
that he proposed t'me.

"you seem t'have quite the relationship
with Arlene wouldn't ya say?"
Johnny questioned intently.

"what's it to ya?
can't quite disclose any information.
th'whole doctor-patient confidentiality thing,"
I stated.

"tell ya what, shit-bag
if you want the remainin' pieces of yer little letter
you can have fun gettin' Arlene t'go out with me
how's that?"
he enticed.

"might wanna try'n find a genie lamp
t'grant ya that wish, pal.
ain't nothin' I can say that's gonna convince her
to go out with yer ugly mug,"
I pressed.

"well, complete the task

an' I'll give ya the remaining pieces all at once,"
he said convincingly
"or I'll burn them all right outside yer cell."

Check.

I huffed an' nodded in agreement
but confidently knew there wasn't much
I could say'er do that would
give Arlene the pleasure in goin' on'a date
with that fucker.

I confided in Bruno later that night
told him what Johnny wanted me t'do
yet confessed I didn't want t'put Arlene through the hassle.

"are you fallin' fer this broad?"
Bruno asked starin' up at the chipped ceiling in our cell.

"pffft,"
I snarled
"I ain't got no feelin's for her
she may be the queen in this game
but she's jus' as expendable as any other pawn."

"you makin' her sound like she's untouchable.
if I recall, the queen protects the king
at all costs, ya?
might wanna start usin' her t'produce results
is all I'm sayin'."

The fuck was I thinking

protectin' Arlene like that?
what the fuck was wrong with me?

I sounded like a fuckin' pussy
all soft'n juicy for this woman
who hadn't yet made herself useful t'me
an' it was 'bout time to put her promises
t'the test.

"You said you wanted to help me

an' I need yer help."

"what does a gal get in return?"
Arlene pressured.

"a piece'a the pie.
the piece that helps exact my revenge.
if ya wanna be part'a this story
now's the time to commit
or sit an' watch it unfold."

she put her finger to her lips
tappin' them like a metronome
as her thought process deepened
b'fore she answered
"I'll do it."

"you don't even know what I'm gonna ask ya,"
I countered.

"you said it'd be worth it.
consider this my commitment."

Hook, line and sinker

she heard my plan
bought my plan
but found a flaw—
the whole plan was shit.

"Bruno'n I thought this through
how can ya say the plan is shit?
it's full proof!"
I exclaimed.

"Sugar, I trusted you
now it's time you go and trust me.
I'll take care of the big boy for you
and I'll get the rest of that letter,"
she winked.

Wait a minute…

I know what yer thinkin'

who just baited who?

Needless to say

Bruno wasn't so fond'a the new plan
"trust her?
we barely know'r!
what if she goes'n tells Johnny?
you lettin' yer feelings for this broad cloud yer judgement."

"now wait a minute.
she been leadin' on 'bout helpin' us
an' somethin' gives me a feelin' she wants to,"
I defended.

"yah, yer feelin' all weak in the knees fer her
jus' like ev'ry other pussy-whipped sum-bitch in here,"
Bruno declared.

"you better watch yer tongue.
jus' b'cause we friends don't make me obligated
t'take you outta here with me.
yer not even blood."

Bruno harassed
"you wanna kill yer blood.
somethin' tells me
bein' your friend is better."

The tension died out

like'a car runnin' outta gas
as we both calmed our minds
wit the cool breeze blowin' over our skin.

I saw where he was comin' from
playing that devil's advocate
secretly and consciously remindin' me
t'keep my eye on the prize
an' not get distracted by petty emotions.

Love is petty

when it first sticks to a person.
it latches on like a leech
suckin' a person 'til they've been bled dry.

dry of money.
dry of words.
dry of spontaneity.
dry of emotions.
dry of selflessness.

love is revenge
that isn't just a dish
best served cold
but served swiftly an' just
while we take out our
missed love
on
found love
and call it passion.

Did I love Arlene?

no.

but I'd lead her on t'believe so
'cause the only thing stronger than love is

passion.

Arlene kept good on her promise though

showin' up on Johnny's double shift
wearin'a sleek dress
auburn in color that stretched right b'low her knees.
a pair'a flats wit little bowties on top
that brushed the marble floors
soundin' like'a bird flappin' its wings in the wind.
her raspberry blonde hair curled
bouncin' like springs wit every step she took
catchin' the eye an' dick of ev'ry man in that prison.

seduction was her method.
one she excelled at I'll admit
b'cause if you got gay men lookin' in yer direction
wit a pair of knockers as large as hers
red lipstick that popped like'a fire hydrant
and an ass that curved like rollin' hilltops
I'd call that God's gift t'men.

But in that moment

she weren't no gift t'us men
jus' to one
an' like every other man
that would'a pounced on her like a bag of catnip
Johnny Boy was lured no differently
as Arlene played little miss innocent.

coercing him t'follow her t'her office quickly
she played him like a fiddle
in jus' a few short minutes
perfecting the simplest task that would
grant me my prize.

the chatter among the men was low
as faint sounds an' moans were heard
with one shadow present
from the shade drawn door window.

b'fore long some rustling happened
an' out came Arlene
explainin' she had'a conference to attend.
she weren't the only one that came
as Johnny exited the office
bucklin' his belt wit the face of relief.

No sooner did Arlene leave

I approached Johnny
"I made good on my promise.
better than a date wouldn't ya agree?"

"saved me a bunch of sweet talkin' bullshit
that's fer sure,"
Johnny adjusted himself
makin' it a point for me to notice
"here's your stupid paper.
hope you enjoy it,"
he cackled as he walked away.

The crumbled bits of paper

were torn into even smaller pieces than the previous ones
as I filtered them out on my bed.
Bruno came closer t'help me.

it were worse than any puzzle I'd ev'r solved
havin' no picture t'compare it to
an' not knowin' what it'd say.

in no time though
letters started t'form

        G

   S
O   F

     E
            U
  Y
                  R

until a simple sentence formed...
And then it was clear

the letter wasn't the brothers' at all
rather, it was Johnny's
that read:

GO
FUCK
YOURSELF.

THE PAST

"Wake up son of mine,"

were the soft words my mother'd speak t'me
in the mornin's t'get me outta bed.

her voice was like silk
wrappin' my body like a hug
slippin' ov'r me wit comfort an' ease.
sometimes she'd sit there an' watch me rest exclaimin'
"it's not every day you watch an angel sleep."

I was embarrassed
jus' before she'd kiss my forehead
pat me on the leg an' say
"today's a new day
let's start it off the right way!"

the right way t'start any day fer her
was eggs'n bacon
wit a side'a toast an' small bowl of fruit.

but ev'rything tasted better when she made it
'cause she 'cooked it wit love'
she'd proclaim.

I dare say

back then was 'bout the only time
I ever felt an emotion
despite the hatred I had fer my father.

hate was'a reaction t'his presence
that I gone'n learned from my mother.
not that I remember when
but at some point she started t'hate him
an' let's jus' say it rubbed off on t'me.

'course I saw it here'n there
snippets of discontent
oozin' out the pores'a my mother's skin
detestin' the tears she'd shed
b'cause she felt trapped like a soldier in an ambush
wit nowhere t'go
yet holdin' on t'that last grenade
waitin' fer the enemy t'draw near
where she wouldn't go down without'a fight
takin' as many as she could with'r sacrifice.

But that ambush was a man

an' that grenade were a child
yet she never knew she'd win the war
even when the battle was lost.

Mother's brother was a lover

t'many women an' men.
guy had his wires crossed somewhere
but 'round the time'a mother's passin'
he gone'n settled down wit a little petite thing
who mother referred to as
'the whore'.

called her the whore b'cause
back in high school she fucked my father
an' he always seemed t'eye her
when she'd come ov'r fer dinner.

sure, mother were likely jealous
but the way he and uncle Nick
would joke 'bout double teamin' her
t'keep it in the family
mother'd overhear an' scoff.

I listened in on one of their conversations once

"hey Jim
what's you say we bring Margarette
out t'the shed and have'r strip fer us?
then when she's all naked we spring on her,"
uncle Nick stated.

"let's wait 'til Jill goes t'sleep,"
my father persuaded.

but jus' as their conversation ended
uncle Nick caught me peekin' from 'round the corner
stood up from his chair
"hey, why don't I tuck the boy in t'bed
get some'a that dad practice in?
never know when I'll get the same title as ya
ha ha."

"yeah, sure. jus' let Jill know,"
father stated unhindered.

Walking up the steps to my room

uncle Nick was close b'hind
so close that his hand smacked my ass
tellin' me to "git goin' now, don't have all night."

I got in my room an' started t'undress
but uncle Nick jus' stood in my doorway
his hand slidin' up the molding
grippin' it tightly like he would his dick
watchin' me intently.

he started t'unbutton his flannel shirt
right b'fore my mother approached from b'hind him
"Nick, make sure you read him a bedtime story."

He read me a story alright

wit my door closed
lights off
holdin' his half naked body close t'mine
an' his hand over my mouth.

he whispered in t'my ear
"you scream—i'll kill you.
you tell anyone—i'll kill you.
you jus' lay still now
let uncle Nick take good care of you."

"Did he molest you?"

Arlene asked sincerely.

"yup. the fucker sure did.
an' not just that once,"
I added.

"did your mother ever find out?"

"I think she had'a suspicion
that uncle Nick were'a boy lover
but it nev'r came t'fruition b'fore she died."

"how did your mother die, Michael?"
Arlene asked wit desperation.

"now, now, we mustn't get ahead'a ourselves.
ya gotta hear the story
b'fore you can see the man."

"but I see the man.
I just need the story to understand the man,"
she concluded.

"you see what I want you t'see."

"Well then why don't you tell me about Bruno,"

Arlene insisted
changin' subjects all chameleon like.

"what 'bout him?"

"when did y'all meet?"
she asked diligently.

"on the outside
when we's were young.
didn't b'come friends right away though."

"oh. why's that?"

"ah, well our paths cross'd again later in life
'bout the time we both seemed t'be gettin' in trouble,"
I tittered.

Arlene clicked'r pen an' started t'write
"why didn't you become friends right away though?"
she asked.

"didn't need each other I'd guess.
small town
can't like ev'ryone in it.
let's jus' say we both recognized
we needed each other at the same time.
after that we got t'be partners in crime
havin' similar goals."

"so, Bruno wants to kill his father too?"
she questioned while studyin' my face.

"Bruno don't have no father,"
I stated aggressively.

Arlene went an' jotted some more notes b'fore concluding

"ya know, I'd rather get t'know him
with his own words
not just the tales you tell of him."

"I assure you
they ain't no tales.
but no promises he'll come."

Upon my exit from her office
her warm touch glided down my arm
as she stopped me
"I forgot to tell you I'm sorry."

"I told ya I don't need yer sympathy."

"no, no, Sugar, about the letter.
thought we had it."

We?

I thought walkin' back t'my cell.
what was this 'we' talk?

there was no
we
or
us
or
together.

it was
me
and
myself
and
I.

Back in the cell Bruno was waiting

an' I could tell he were gettin' anxious
'cause his tell was always the way
he'd pick his cuticles.
he'd push the extra skin down
an' then stretch it up the nail
makin' a flab'a skin that he'd then
chew on
sof'enin' the skin b'fore he'd grab a far end
then tear it wit his teeth.
sometimes it'd bleed
an' he'd look at the blood
lettin' it leak outta his finger
jus' before he'd lick it up
tastin' the metal-like flavor.

He looked on at me

"if I had'a watch
I'd be tappin' it,"
he boldly stated.

"listen here
I'm workin' the angles.
we gotta be patient…"

Bruno interrupted
"I think you wanna stay in here."

"the fuck you mean?"
I questioned.

"let's find out."

Bruno got up off his bed

an' proceeded past me
stormin' out like he were a twister
wrapped up'n headin' for disaster.

I tried catchin' up t'him
but his pace was steady like a stallion
'til he reached Arlene's office door.

grippin' the doorknob
he barely even turned it b'fore pushin' the door in
"woman!"
he spoke loudly
"I think it's time we met."

Arlene were startled while she looked past Bruno
straight at me standin' in the doorway
"Michael…"

Bruno cut her off
"I'm your patient now.
forget Michael fer a minute
b'cause I got some questions."

Arlene's look was curious yet confused.
she put down the paperwork she'd been holdin'
an' found a comfy ledge t'lean against
starin' deep in t'Bruno's eyes
"Bruno is it?"
she asked kindly.

"yes'm."

"I'm glad to have finally met you.
Michael has told me
much about you and your friendship,"
she exclaimed with joy.

"listen
let's cut t'the chase here.
we have'a mission
t'get outta here an' I jus' gotta know
are ya gonna help us'r not?"

"well, Bruno
that's not an easy task to accomplish.
someone in my position doesn't have the access
or knowledge on how to get prisoners out,"
her tone began to change
"but I know the reasons for which I want to help, Michael…
can't say I know yours."

"from what I hear
you ain't convinced yet t'help him.
as fer my reasons
I vowed t'help Michael long ago
in helpin' him kill his father
b'cause the man has ev'ry reason t'do so."

Arlene reached for her notebook on the table next t'her.
she started t'write a few things b'fore she responded
"you're an aggressive one.
and I know there's no getting around you.
so I'll tell you what…"

Bruno began t'talk ov'r her
"I'll tell you what, miss
you say right here
right now
yer gonna help the two'a us get outta here.
I'll worry 'bout how
Michael will worry 'bout why
an' you jus' worry 'bout what I tell ya."

"I'm failing to see what's in this for me,"
Arlene rebutted.

"satisfaction."

"the satisfaction of what?"
she inquired.

"helpin' Michael achieve his goal."

After a moment

Arlene gave a nod
that symbolized all the chips were in.

we were gonna beat the house
an' we were gonna take all the players wit us.

'cause not every game is played t'win
some are played t'watch everyone else lose.

"That's how it's done,"

Bruno patted me on the back
as we walked out t'the courtyard to smoke.

"had ya jus' given me a little more time…"
I muttered.

"you have the broad by the wet panties
she sits in ev'ry time she talks t'ya.
give her the story she want's t'hear
an' get her on board fully."

He was right

I had been draggin' my feet
tryin' t'make the story more profound
but there was no need fer that
the story was true

an' the truth sets us free.

The truth was this:

I was seven years old when my mother died.

she were murdered.

my father killed her in our house in th'summer of '53.

an' he got away with it.

RYAN A. KOVACS

I WAS SEVEN

So here's the story

you been waitin' t'hear.
It ain't pleasant
it ain't exaggerat'd
an' it sure as shit ain't gonna change you
the way it changed me.

It were July 8th

an' the summer sun raged like a fire
heatin' up our Texas estate
like our land was bein' cooked on'a grill.

The mornin' is mostly a blur
but the mos' important part of it was the screaming.
My mother'd been up since the rooster crowed
an' my father b'fore that.
Mother nev'r seemed t'be in a hurry wit anything she did
since she always seem'd t'plan ahead.
Her motto was
'if you fail to plan
ya plan to fail.'

The sayin' was kinda like glue t'me
stickin' wit me all these years now
but it took me too damn long t'figure it out
that preparedness were ev'rything.

Truth be told however

there wasn't a fuckin' thing that could prepare me
fer that day
layin' in my bed
lookin' out the window at the orange glare
feelin' the season's heat rise from the ground
as it blew through my room.

Downstairs I heard the back door slam
as mild voice tones echoed through the floorboards
an' upon reachin' my ears
had erupted in t'thunderous roars.
I glided outta bed
creepin' down the stairs
listening t'the voices of my mother and father
bickerin' 'bout I don't remember
'til I reached the corner of the kitchen doorway
starin' at my mother in disbelief.

She stood there with hate in her eyes

graspin' a knife from the drawer she hadn't yet closed
pointing it right at my father's heart.

"I'm leaving you, James!
An' I'm taking Michael with me!"
mother yelled.

Father moved in rapidly
as he whack'd the knife from mother's hand
sendin' it flying t'wards my feet
while he began t'pummel my mother wit his fists.

Unable t'control my emotions
I did what I could to protect my mother
steadily grabbin' the knife
an' walkin' up b'hind my father
screamin' for him to stop.

My mother with little strength spoke
"Michael go back t'your room, honey."

But she couldn't hide what my eyes had seen—
the brutality of father's intentions.

"You threatening me boy?"

father asked outraged.
His eyes resembled a tiger
glossy t'the point of appearin' as glass
yet completely full wit ill intent.

Mother tried t'say more
but he gone'n hit her in the stomach
stealin' the breath from'r words.
He snarled once more
"boy, I asked you a fuckin' question!"
expectin' an answer from me
"you better drop that knife right now
or so help me
I'll kill yer mother right here!"

I dropped the knife

as the blade an' handle danced
back'n forth
end ov'r end
like a pair'a dancers doin' a waltz
'til it came to a ringing end
of vibrating metal an' wood.

Father approached me
wrappin' his rugged hands 'round my throat
pushin' me 'gainst the kitchen wall
an' raising me with one hand
until we were eye level.

I was chokin' and frantically kickin' and punchin' the air
while his grip tightened 'round my neck
as he spoke
"if yer gonna threaten a man
ya better be ready to carry out that threat."

The alcohol on his breath

was old'n bitter
with bags under his eyes indicatin'
he'd nev'r slept that night.

Mother begged'm to put me down
'til no sooner did he drop me
he pick'd the knife up from the ground
turnin' the tables on mother
pointin' the blade at her heart.

"you lousy excuse of a family
how dare y'all bite the hand that feeds you!"

he struck fear in t'mother's heart with jus' a look
as he proceeded to turn me ov'r
placing my coughin' limp body 'cross his bent knee
pullin' my pajama pants down
exposing my ass cheeks
while he began t'spank me
with'n open palm
an' calloused skin
until I had…

Red biscuits.

Two little buns
beaten
whipped
an'
stingin' hot
as I cried
an' gagged on absent air.

Throwing me to the ground

after my ass cheeks were as red as lava
an' stingin' like I'd sat on a stovetop
father calmly stood up
and wit no remorse concluded
"betray me again
an' I'll kill ya both,"
as he spit on the wooden floor
exitin' out the back door.

Through my sobbing

I heard mother mutt'r under her breath
"not if I kill you first."

The day proceeded

as usual an' carefree as a day could.
The actions of the mornin' became a remnant
come th'evening when
the devil and the lord fought for three souls.

An' God did not win.

The shotgun rang

like a triumphant clap'a thunder
where I felt my body jolt
as if the lightnin' that followed
had struck me in my bed.
Pullin' the covers ov'r my head
I began t'hear runnin' feet climb the wooden stairs.

My door flung open
an' the light switch
sprung upwards like'a paddle ball.

Mother slammed the door shut
clickin' the lock
then began t'shake me sayin'
"wake up son of mine
your mama got somethin' t'tell you!"

I pulled the sheet off my face
seein' the fear and uncertainty in her eyes
as she went on
"son, your father is a bad man.
He don't deserve us
an' he wants us dead.
I'm going to protect you
but should I fail
you gots t'remember one important thing.
If you wanna survive in this here world
you gotta keep the heart cold
b'cause it's easier to warm it up."

Ripping me from my bed

she pushed me in t'my closet
throwin' my white bed sheet ov'r my head an' body
"you stay hidden here
no matter what ya hear
and close your eyes so you can be invisible.
Take this knife fer your protection
an' should anyone open this closet door
you just stab until you can't no more.

I love you, Michael."

As soon as she shut the door

I could hear mother inch outside my room
b'fore the shotgun click
reloaded a round in the chamber.
Her unexpected cry of terror
sent shivers down my spine as I heard her words
"stay back!
I won't let you hurt this family no more
you son-of-a bitch!"

I honed in on the meticulous squeeze'a the trigger
which tick'd like'a clock hand
that sounded a
loud
roaring
thundering
conquering
silence
into the air.

My bedroom door burst open

like a hurricane'd tore through the house
rippin' it off its hinges
as grunts an' thrusts of hands an' feet
pushed air into thuds.

"you fuckin' bitch!
I'll fuckin' kill you!"

I could hear mother fight father off'a her
clawin' at his face
while smacks emitted rhythmic static
like that of'a record player.

Seconds felt like hours while
I refined my ears t'listen in
on the struggle that took place
jus' inches away from my body.

But I couldn't take it any longer

my mother was suffering
unable t'hold her own
as I envisioned father's overpowering strength
stealin' the life from'r.

through the slits on my closet door
I could see a figure hoverin' ov'r another
that practically laid limp on the ground.

I thought t'myself

I won't let him kill her.
   I won't let him win.
           I have to kill him.

Like a surge of electricity

I rushed out from my closet
my eyes clenched tight like'a sailors knot
the bed sheet my cloak of invisibility
an' knife firmly gripped b'tween both my half-pint hands
rememberin' my mother's sayin'
'blade t'the sky'
as I thrusted deep and unyielding into flesh.

I screamed wit rage'n fury
jabbin' the blade in an' out of each new wound I created
while warm blood splatter'd the bed sheet
soaking my face.

Finally, my body fell t'the side
as I grew tired and weak in the knees
which gave sight t'the dirtied apron
my mother always wore.

Removing the sheet from my body
I stared in disbelief
as blood poured from my mother's backside
drenchin' my father's clothes beneath her.

I dropped the knife to the floor

but this time it did not bounce or dance
echoin' the terrors of my own reality.
No.
this time it fell flat an' didn't move
like the body it had jus' help mangle.

Starin' at my mother's corpse
tears began t'well in my eyes
as father slowly inched away
an' leaned 'gainst my bed.

By the time it became clear
none of it made any sense.

The shotgun on the floor in the hall—
the empty shell last fired not ejected—
my father wit'a gunshot wound t'the shoulder—
his blood mixin' with my mother's—
the silence that muted us both...

He tricked me into killing my mother

an' he lied 'bout the whole fuckin' story.
Sayin' she tried to kill him and I saved his life.
By the time the cops went t'question me
they'd already had their story
from the man who threatened me wit what t'say.

Not long after
he gone'n gave me t'my uncle fer adoption
so he could go start'a new life without th'one he killed.

He never looked back
an' quite frankly
neither did I.

The silence was heavy in the room

heavy 'nough t'measure it
yet unable t'lift it.

Arlene looked on at me
wit discontent an' incredulity
at the story that unfolded from my mouth
filterin' words an' images in t'her runnin' mind.

She looked on at me
"Michael…"

"I told ya I didn't need no sympathy
so keep that shit at bay,"
I in'erjected.

"I'm sorry, it's just that
it's such a horrific story
so painful to imagine
a child going through that…
you going through that."

Arlene began t'clear her throat b'fore she continued
"but you've given me insight
and understanding as to why
you want to kill your father.
It sounds satisfying to say now
that I'm willing to help you achieve your goal
and however I am able to help
in whatever capacity
I will.
Your father deserves to suffer for his crime, Sugar
so let's find him
        and kill him."

"He's not going to be the only casualty,"

I added
"there are others who stand in my way."

As Arlene finished writin' a note in'r notebook
she looked up at me wit growin' contempt
an' professed

"we'll kill them all."

THE WAY OUT

While I'm sure you may have guessed

there were only one way outta that prison
an' the details 'bout it were clear
that ev'ry resource would need t'be exhausted.

lies would be told
betrayal inevitable
favors cashed in
goods owed
an' all angles covered.

Bruno an' I laid out the plan
like we were'a bunch of grunts
usin' sticks an' rocks'n
anything that could be used fer representation
of the obstacles'n people
we'd need t'overcome.

while some obstacles would be
more difficult than others
Pete'n re-Pete assur'd us
escape were possible.

"you two can come wit us
if this all goes down as planned,"
I affirmed.

Pete chuckled b'fore his brother spoke up
"we are right where we wanna be.
an' as long as you make good on yer promise
we'll keep ya well hidden from the world."

Them boys were simpletons

havin' the only favor to repay them be
to spread lies 'bout the U.S. an' Soviet Union.
propaganda was their greatest weapon
in a world'a suckers'n credulous sheep
blindly obeyin' and believing ev'rything spoken
were nothin' but the truth.

they knew it'd only be a matter a'time b'fore
the world would crumble'n society would burn
an' they didn't care 'bout money
they didn't care 'bout fame
they simply wanted human nature t'create chaos
so they could sit idly by an' laugh at its destruction.

The collective effort

was seemingly enough ov'r the course
of the followin' two weeks.

Arlene made good on'r temptations t'wards Johnny
convincin' his pecker it'd get wet
an' his mind she actually liked'm.
she certainly was a heartbreaker
but that was part'a the plan.
all the pieces were lining up
an' my advancement t'wards my end goal
was close in sight.

In our final session

as patient an' subject
I questioned her on the plan
double checkin' t'see if she knew her role.

"after we make it out the front gate
you gotta keep Johnny Boy distracted
so we can bag'm an' high tail it outta there.
you gonna be able t'keep it t'gether?"

"Sugar, I know what to do."

my mind traveled somewhere fer a moment
that made me ask'n ardent question
"why are ya doin' this fer me?"

an' without any hesitation she spoke
"because I love you."

The day had arrived

that my victory was near.
inside I was nothin' but a caged animal
trapp'd b'hind bars that granted me only sight.

a vision of perspective that soon became my reality
where my freedom would not be free
yet come wit the greatest costs
I had ev'ry intention of payin'.

Arlene seemed to have materialized

out of thin air
while no one in that prison expected her
on'a Friday afternoon.
half the men were takin' naps
while the rest were concealed
in either the courtyard or fields.
wit ev'ryone spread out
it'd be hours b'fore they'd notice two men disappear'd
an' since Johnny made his own fuckin' schedule
no one'd be wiser t'his absence none.

Her timing was impeccable

jus' as Johnny got up t'go to the bathroom.
she came in wearin' a lengthy coat
sleek as the hood of'a '57 chevy
wit high heels that clacked
like an axe on wood.

she didn't even mutter a word to'm
as Johnny begged the other guard
t'cover his shift for awhile.
her look was fierce
an' filled with much intent
that he were blinded to
while her actions spoke louder than words ev'r could.

from there the two proceeded t'her car
parked jus' outside the gate
where our getaway was fast an' precise
while the hand inside the honeypot were now stuck.

Bruno and I started moving

down the corridor t'wards Harry's cell
where upon meetin' him
Bruno laid out a mockin' gesture wit his hand
instigatin' distaste fer an excuse t'start a commotion.
Harry stood from his bed
like he'd been woken suddenly by noise
an' approached Bruno
to which Bruno gone'n grabbed his four fingers
liftin' his arm high 'bove his own shoulder
flexin' the fingers down
jus' b'fore he bent them t'touch the back of Harry's hand.

Harry screamed like he'd been kicked in the balls
an' no sooner
Bruno then forced his elbow t'wards the sky
creatin'a compound fracture
almost making Harry piss himself wit pain.

upon our exit
Harry laid there clenchin' his arm
bellowin' from distress an' pleadin' fer help
b'fore the two guards near the hall had moved
an' Pete waved us down t'proceed.

Our exit was swift

and our movements cat-like
but our position 'bout t'be known
as the one thing we hadn't accounted fer
was standin' b'tween us an' the exit.

Bruno tensed up as we came to a halt
seein' six guards on their union break
sippin' hot coffee an' jerking 'round wit each other.
our presence was known
an' we were where we shouldn't have been
while the guards all looked at us
concerned'n curious.

re-Pete was in position
but his brother gave'm a look t'hold
as Bruno an' I formulated a mental plan t'gether
by actin' on the obstacle b'fore us.

Bruno charged like he were a bull

seein' nothing but red ahead of 'm
as he began t'paint the brick walls
wit the color of their insides.
there were no sense in gettin' in his way
since the man could not be stopped.
his motive was t'kill
to be the manifestation of death itself
wit no chains t'hold'm back
seein' only one objective—
t'get out.

While I paint the picture

of Bruno bein' invincible
I assure you, he ain't.
he wasn't some superhero
who never'd been touched
never been injured
nor tempted
comin' out of'a shit storm unscathed.

he was a man
like I said b'fore
an' I told ya not t'forget that.

but this reminder ain't t'tell ya
that despite who he was at that point in time
was no comparison t'what he'd become.

when he charged them guards
he were bloodthirsty
a maniac t'the highest degree
where even the men helpin' us were fearful.

he was ev'rything but a man
havin' no thoughts
no cares
an' no mortal ties t'the world.
even if the world wanted t'take him on
he woulda stood victorious.

And victorious he was in that moment

as he stood there
wit bruises from
fists that beat his face
batons that hammered his forearm
feet that kicked his sides
heads that bashed his chin
bricks that pounded his back
an' blood that soaked his clothes
wit six men

d i s m e m b e r e d

diStraUghT
     defeate d
           e
           a
           d.

his breathin' was labored
b'fore he sighed wit release
nodding t're-Pete t'open the door.

Pete stood b'side me
whisperin' in my ear
"that was insane."

as the door t'the free world started t'open
I spoke coldly
"that was nothin'."

Upon our escape

I shook the brother's hands
thanking them fer all their troubles
and promisin' t'uphold my end of the bargain.

the courtyard was practically empty
b'sides the pansies pushin' up daisies on the bench.

but before long
our approach t'the final gate
wit the final guard
standin' b'tween us an' freedom
the alarm began t'sound
an' urgency was at hand.

to remain hidden
Bruno stood outside the guard shack
waitin' fer his opportunity
as the guard exited rapidly
gun in hand
only t'be met wit a fist t'his face
that immediately sent teeth flying
as he stutter stepped backwards
smashin' the window on the door
wit the butt stock'a the rifle.
Bruno then grabbed the man's head
an' slid it 'cross the shards of glass stickin' up
slicin' his carotid artery.
we didn't have time t'listen to the man gurgle his life away
as I hit the button t'unlock the gate door.

But the departure was met with hilarity

where Arlene's car were parked
jus' a few yards away
wit the backdoor open
two legs spread open like barn doors
firmly planted in the gravel
an' Johnny Boy hoverin' ov'r her
payin' no mind t'the alarm blaring
from inside the prison.

Arlene had made good on her promise

as I snuck up b'hind Johnny
his pants piled at his feet
bare ass t'the wind
grabb'd his baton that'd been strategically placed
on the roof 'a the car
an' gave him a taste of his own damn medicine
windin' up nice'n wide
wit'a rigid stance
yellin' out t'him
"hey, Johnnyyyyy…"

he turned t'look at me
an' jus' as we made blissful eye contact
I clobber'd the side of his face wit ev'rything I had
sendin' his limp body'n hard dick
right t'the fuckin' ground.

Just as Johnny fell

Arlene looked up at me
briefly startled but still in the moment
an' asked me
if I wanted t'finish what Johnny started
as she gently began t'rub her inner thighs.

"ain't got time fer that right now.
we best get movin' and fast."

placin' Johnny's body in the trunk
hands'n feet bound by the rope Arlene'd brung
the dust trail in our wake had simmer'd
as we departed the prison
by the slow drizzle of rain that started up.

wit the windshield wipers on
closin' in on the nearest highway
Arlene asked as she drove
"where we headed, Sugar?"

"the nearest rail yard."

RYAN A. KOVACS

DAUNTING
SATISFACTION

"I know what yer thinking right now

an' it's okay t'think that.
it's a difficult answer for anyone
who finds themselves in a position such as yers
but trust me when I tell ya
it will be ov'r as quick as you allow it.
you see, the only problem we face right now
is that you have somethin' I want
somethin' I need
an' the catch is that
I can't hear you wit them fingers in your mouth.
I happen t'know how painful torture can be
so I gave ya somethin' t'bite down on
t'help subdue the pain you'll suffer.
as soon as ya bite them fingers off however
the pain will stop
an' you'll be able t'tell me what I need t'hear.
I know it's a simple answer
'cause them brothers who gave me that note
you so graciously read
an' tricked me in t'believin'
was bein' torn up b'fore me

they only wrote necessities.

ya may not know this
but the location on that paper
was the whereabouts of my father...

the man I've sworn t'kill.

now let me assure you
had you not fucked wit me
I'd have left your carcass back at the prison
'long wit all the rest'a the guards
an' be on my way t'meet him
instead'a bein' sidetracked wit you.
but here we are

in my playhouse now
where I hold the power instead of you.
believe me when I tell ya
the only shred'a hope lies within you
an' once I have what I need
you'll be free t'go

Arlene will make sure'a that."

Johnny tried t'say somethin'
that came out like gurgles.

"shhhh, shhhhh, shhhhh.
it's okay, it's okay.
I'll try not to enjoy this as much
as you enjoyed bashin' me ov'r the head
breakin' my fingers
beatin' me for no mother-fucking reason at all
an' suckerin' me into readin' yer farce letter.
but I can't make any promises.

so here's how this is gonna work, Johnny Boy.
as you may have already noticed
there's a noose 'round yer neck
an' that's there for insurance.
you're balancin' on one leg
that's literally preventing you from chokin' yerself
an' you'll have t'maintain that
throughout the duration of however long this takes.

but over here I gots myself a sledgehammer
an' if you're familiar
wit the human anatomy
you might be seein' where I'm goin' wit this."

I held the long wooden handle
lettin' it sway in m'hand like a pendulum.

"the top'a the foot is connected

t'yer tibia and fibula bones
which at this very moment
are the most vital bones t'yer survival
since yer standin' on'em.
while you may have two legs
I could be bashin' instead'a one
time's against us both an' I need results quickly.

now, here's how this is gonna go fer you, ya piece of shit.
my sledge hammer's gonna have
6 blissful swings
in the event I don't miss
fer you to bite them fingers'a yers off
t'tell me the location of my father.
I don't care what ya do wit them fingers none
swallow 'em
spit 'em out
or tuck 'em in the corners of yer mouth like tobacco.

jus' make sure I hear ya loud'n clear
b'cause ya only got five toes
an' once I make it to the whole foot
yer gonna wanna tell me what I wanna hear
b'cause that's where my insurance come in.

ya see, if it comes down to it
an' I shatter the foot you be standin' on
yer whole leg is gonna collapse
like a house'a cards
an' that rope 'round yer neck
gonna be a permanent necklace
which will force yer lower jaw t'bite
and hard mind you
ultimately givin' us both our desired outcome—

your pain fer my pleasure.

so the faster you understand
how serious this matter is

the easier it'll be fer you t'walk outta here.
no pun intended."
I snicker'd t'myself.

"here we go.

                          are ya ready?"

CASE #127 - MICHAEL ENNIS (NOTES):

First session with Michael today.
Seems like he is playing coy with me.
Didn't bring Bruno with him.
Bruno doesn't do well in closed in spaces? (claustrophobia?)
Michael does?
How are the two men connected?
Why'd I call him Sugar?
Didn't ask for sexual favors.
Quite flirtatious.

Wants something but don't know what.

I could see the look in Johnny's eyes

the terror he were feelin'
as I inched clos'r t'him movin' the sledgehammer
to'n fro
as it begged my hands
t'crush his petty toes.

Arlene leaned 'gainst the car
where jus' minutes ago she begged me t'stop
as I tied Johnny up
in his jackknife position
tryin' t'convince me there would be
some other way t'make him talk.
when I shut her down
slammin' m'fists on the hood of the car
Johnny woke from his daze
jus' as soon as Arlene started t'get the hint
that nothin' beyond that point would be pleasant.

"please, Michael
there must be another way,"
Arlene pleaded for Johnny Boy.

"listen t'me good when I tell ya
this is the monster you set free.
this is the monster you swore t'help.
if he scares you
I suggest you leave.
but I told you
many'a times now
nothin' would stop me from killin' my father
an' this man knows where he is."

"why couldn't ya just ask the brothers
what the note said?"

"when a man goes outta his way
t'give you a favor

ya don't go back askin' for the same favor
b'cause ya fucked up the first one,"
I announced.

"but it wasn't your fault
that you lost the letter they wrote you.
Johnny took it from you,"
Arlene tried t'resolve.

"now it's my time
t'take somethin' from him."

Of course she wasn't aware

that, that was the plan all along
which Bruno'n I agreed she needed t'be
in the dark 'bout
'cause the odds were
had she known
her commitment may not have been
to the fullest capacity
despite her acceptance t'kill ev'ryone
who'd get in my way.
sure, she said it
but did she mean it?

not likely b'cause
as sure as shit, there we were
bickerin' about the means in which
I would extract information
an' yet, havin' it questioned
in the manner in which I'd provide it
while Johnny looked on
findin' what he would believe
was the chink in our armor.

but when she came t'the conclusion
that I were not budgin'
it sure as shit b'came abundantly clear t'her
that the only way Johnny Boy were talkin'
was through pain.

Let's clarify

usually speakin'
the ones that act tough
ain't.

obviously, we should all know
the exception t'that rule by now.

however, jus' as the old sayin' goes
'all bark no bite'
Johnny Boy was gonna need t'bite
in order t'bark fer me.

And bark he did

wit the first swing'a the sledgehammer
that came crashin' down on his pinkie toe
flattening it like a penny on'a railroad track
jus' after a train'd run over it.

his yelp was like hearin' a pig
runnin' in its pen havin' nowhere t'go.

I grew excited
"damn I got good aim!
ya know how hard it is
t'just hit that small toe
wit this big ass piece'a metal?"

Arlene was far from amused
as she had a look of distaste on'r face.
Bruno gave a small grin
while he sat wit the passenger door open
smokin' a cig.

He was generous enough

t'grant me the opportunity
of torturin' Johnny
since he fuck'd wit me more than him
but there wasn't nothin' I'd do t'stop him
if he wanted t'interfere.

the sidelines weren't always where Bruno
preferred t'be an' quite frankly
I can't blame'm.
the man had endured much in his years
an' there wasn't much in life
that gave him satisfaction
like makin' other people feel pain.
it was likely his favorite thing
an' considerin' he didn't feel pain
one could say
he projected the very thing he didn't feel
onto those who did.

Regardless of the projection of pain however

Johnny's pain stood out more than my pleasure
an' while he appeared t'be losin' focus
I reminded him once more

"don't focus on yer toe
remember what I told ya
the fingers, Johnny Boy
the fingers.
they're the goal
not the pain.
so bite'm off
an' tell me what I need t'hear."

I gave him a brief moment
t'contemplate the pain in his foot
ov'r the fingers in his mouth
an' while multiple decisions
likely passed through his mind
his seconds must've felt like hours
until I wound up once more
strikin' the next two toes.

"oh shit.
my bad.
I missed
an' took two at once.
guess my aim were off,"
I stated disheartened.

Like a pair of ketchup packets

Johnny's three toes lied flat
wit red splatter jettin' out in each direction.
his agony was almost t'the sound of 'a tune
as his breathin' were heavy
an' his moans cavernous.

Arlene shouted
"Johnny!
just bite your fucking fingers off already!
he's not messing around with you
this is serious."

"listen t'the pretty lady
she's come to the realization
and so should you.
at least show some effort man,"
I instigated.

CASE #127 - MICHAEL ENNIS (NOTES CONTINUED):

Michael's file is filled mostly with crime.
Not much on his childhood, record starts in teens.
Family was murdered, mother, uncle and aunt.
No case notes on murders.
Father lived, but unknown whereabouts.
No education but seems educated? (he reads books—precocious child perhaps?)

Wants to get out of prison… (to kill his father! why?)

It's clear to think

that I've gone mad
that I'm some psychopath
who is on a blood seekin' rampage
strictly fer revenge.
but I dare guess
that you're interested
that the danger excites ya
that you're wonderin' where this all leads
or if I'll let you down at the end.

the end you so patiently wait t'read
t'see if yer expectations are met
an' thirst quenched.

ya see
we aren't so different you'n I
b'cause neither of us
wants me t'fail

an' that makes both of us

mad.

But it feels good to be bad too.

t'go against the grain
t'swim upstream
t'run uphill
t'stand out in the crowd
t'be diff'rent than all the rest.

b'cause ain't no one can stop ya
if they can't find you
when yer goin' yer own way without 'em.

"Johnny, Johnny, Johnny,"

I pressed
"there comes a time when'a man
has t'look at himself
an' ask that silly question
what if I'd done this
or done that
an' I sure do hope yer 'bout there
b'cause yer running out of toes
an' them last two are precious."

I got down on one knee
gazin' at the splattered masterpiece I'd created
wit my sledge as my brush
an' Johnny's blood as my paint
all sprayed'n scattered
like I'd whisked the brush on the canvas
wit no rhyme'r reason for each careless stroke.

oh, but there were a rhyme
an' there certainly were a reason
that became abundantly clear t'him
as I examined the remainin' toes.

"ya know, my mother always used t'play
the little piggy game wit me.
you must be familiar wit it
but if not, I'd be happy t'enlighten ya."

pointin' at where his pinkie toe used t'be
"see, my mother always used t'start wit the pinkie toe.
she'd say that one went t'the market."
starin' at Johnny's toe
"I think yers got hit by a car on the way.
but then the next one
well, she always said that little piggy stayed home.
an' by the looks of it
yers must've been murdered by the piggy

that didn't get no roast beef!"
I chuckled with slight jubilation.

"while the middle piggy she would exclaim
was the one who got roast beef...
looks t'me like he sure got some,"
as I reached down t'pull the remainin' toe nail
that jetted upwards from the flap of skin
still barely attached t'Johnny's foot
he yelped an' cringed from shooting pain
while attemptin' t'bite down harder on his fingers.

Blood started to ooze

from the side'a his mouth
while he gnashed his teeth into his skin
tearin' away flesh 'til he reached bone
where he stopped
unable t'finish the job an' give me what I desired

"looks like this piggy
still ain't gettin' no roast beef,"
I declared jus' b'fore slammin' the sledge
forcefully in t'the tiny bone
squishin' it like a squirrel on the road
and t'my surprise
lendin' the very hand
Johnny needed
t'bite through them bones.

no pun intended.

His scream was desperate

an' clear of emotion
but full'a blood
lookin' like a cannibal
feastin' on himself
while he choked briefly on two fingers
b'fore spittin'em out on the ground.

I let him breathe
heavy and labored breaths
as he attempt'd t'find a way
t'overcome the torture he'd suffered
while I stared him deep in the eye.

"need I remind ya
the only words that should come out yer mouth
are the location of my father.
anything other than that
is subject t'whether or not that last piggy
goes wee all the way home,"
I assured.

"Texarkana."

my ears puckered at the word.

"you sure?"
I asked timidly.

"yes you piece of shit!
now let me down or so help me…"

I interrupted
"I don't believe yer in any position
t'try an' tell me what t'do.
in fact, it's quite the contrary.
so I suggest ya turn that attitude 'round
an' beg me."

Johnny grunted as Arlene began
t'walk in my direction
"Sugar, he gave you what you wanted
let's let him go
so we can move on to the real prize."

In that moment

Arlene leaned in an' kissed me
grabbin' me by the cheek
pullin' me into her
attemptin' to seduce me
wit her beauty an' charm.

for that one single moment
she had me
all of me
stuck in that kiss that changed

nothing.

Our kiss was atomic

like someone dropped an h-bomb
on our lips.
the pressure an' force that connected us
was magnetic and pulsating
as our eyelids squeezed shut
seein' stars and blackness
'til we released
slowly un-stickin' our eyes
lettin' the coolness flow down t'our fingertips
she opened'r eyes wide
only t'blink repeatedly
havin' them bounce back'n forth
as her breath stuttered.

she gripped me tighter
as if she wanted more
yet givin' less'n less
as her blood pooled 'round my knife
which I'd stuck in her deep below'r rib cage.

On her exhale she asked

"why?"

wit fingers twitchin' an' lips quiverin'
while death began t'pass over her quickly

I had'r fooled into thinkin' I was hers
when truly she were mine.

she wanted t'take away all I ever wanted
in thinkin' she could change'a man like me
but the animal inside can't be tamed wit love
b'cause this heart'a mine is chilled
an' like an iceberg
I only show what's above the surface
when underneath is my true nature an' size.

so 'why' she had to ask
as I replied

"I keep the heart cold
b'cause it's easier t'warm it up.
I've had it the coldest t'wards you
when you tried t'get in my way.
I told you nothin' would stop me from
killin' my father
an' I meant nothing.

not even you."

CASE #127 - MICHAEL ENNIS (NOTES CONTINUED):

Why am I abandoning the basic rules of psychology?
There is something mentally wrong with Michael and yet I keep feeding into him.
Is he delusional?
Is he a psychopath?
Where does this anger he seems to harbor come from?

His desires have me intrigued and at the same time, frightened.

Arlene's body slipped from my grasp

gently slidin' t'the dirt
where her limp corpse made a thud.

Johnny was relatively speechless
while his pain had apparently subsided
wit his stare of disbelief.

I shot him a look
an' a smirk
t'indicate to'm
that he were next.

"now wait a fuckin' minute,"
he began t'plead
"I gave ya what you wanted you son-of-a-bitch!
I don't know what Arlene did t'make ya turn on her
an' so help me if I get outta here
I'm gonna kill you fer what you did t'her
an' to me you piece of shit!
LET ME DOWN!"

"you jus' don't learn do ya.
I got ev'rything I want
an' I don't need you anymore.
Arlene played'r part no diff'rent than you did yers.
I have the location of my father
I'm outta prison
I've no attachments
and nothin' t'hold me back anymore,"
I divulged.

"what if I were lyin' huh?
what if I gave ya the wrong information
you won't know unless you keep me alive,"
Johnny tried t'reason wit me.

my sinister laugh was uncontrollable

"you gave up the right information
b'cause I ain't gonna believe fer one second
you endured all that pain
jus' t'lie to me.
Arlene was yer beacon of hope
the reason you thought you'd live
an' now yer tryin' t'reason wit me
having nothin' t'bargain with
'cause she's dead
an' yer about t'be too."

I paused fer a moment
to unsheathe my last weapon
"while I made ya think you were
the only one who knew the information I sought
I knew the location all along.
this were just fer fun,"
I winked.
"wait, wait, wait
I can help you,"
his breathing increased
while he began t'pant like a dog.

"pleading wit me doesn't forgive you
fer what ya did t'me.
I told ya I was gonna kill ya
an' jus' like you keep your promises
so do I."

I wound up the sledgehammer

holdin' it above my head for a moment
while Johnny Boy screamed in terror.

with one last blow
I struck the top'a his foot
crushin' the bones in t'dust
while the chain reaction happened rapidly
while in my mind's eye
it were like watchin' a story unfold.

the breaking of the metatarsals
caused the weight of his body
t'fall an' crumble like a building collapsing
while the tibia shattered like glass
splinterin' out the front
as the fibula pressed 'gainst his knee
then snapped like a branch
completely destroying the only bit'a hope
Johnny Boy were standin' on.

with the jerk of his body
pushin' down on him from gravity
the noose 'round his neck pulled tight
forcin' his jaw t'bite hard
on the remainin' finger in his mouth
while it lodged itself in the back'a his throat
choking him quicker than the rope.

while he dangled there
persuin' the struggle that would surely not prevail
I thought t'myself
how easy it were t'kill a man
t'feed into the desire an'
the hunger
of blood
an' justice.

oh yes
it was more than satiating
while the sins of life
passed ever so smooth through me.
this were my true nature
my true bein'
who I was t'the core

a man
  a killer
                        a monster.

CASE #127 - MICHAEL ENNIS (NOTES CONTINUED):

Michael has insecurity with homosexuality.
Possibly sexually abused as child?
Certainly despises Johnny.
One of the Pete brothers said they 'found him'? Found who?
Michael exited session and was beaten by Johnny.

Johnny is the piece of shit.

RYAN A. KOVACS

WHEN THE BAD GUY WINS

What is a life worth?

if ya calculate it like a math equation
the answer'd be two.
one mother
plus
one father
t'make
one life.

but when you remove one of the parents
the number decreases
an' if you remove both
the answer is simplified
t'nothin'.

that's what I am
a nothing
a nobody
an' yet that's what makes me
worth somethin' more.

see, I am willing t'give ev'rything
b'cause I gots nothin' t'lose.
I lost who I were
an' the only thing I cared fer
when I slain my mother that day
then proceeded t'walk through life
like nothin' more than a ghost.
a ghost who was
tormented
 abused
  spat on
   walked on
    and taken advantage of
     with innocence stripped away.

you tell me
when a boy has lost his innocence

what does he become?
a product of his own environment?
an empty shell jus' watin' t'crack?
a meaningless passerby who blends in wit the crowd?

no.
he becomes less than all that.
he becomes what he was born t'be

nothing.

an' when yer nothing
you can become anything.

and so I chose t'become a man.
I chose t'become a killer.
but I didn't choose t'become

notorious.

In the car ride to the rail yard

Arlene'n I engaged in our last conversation t'gether.
she was oblivious t'my plan
but I had t'keep'r engaged so no flaw would be seen

"what happened back at the prison?
why were the sirens going off?"
Arlene asked with intrigue.

"plan didn't go quite t'plan.
got caught up at the exit
wit the guards on their break
that wasn't calculated."

she expressed concern
"how'd you get out though?
didn't think the Pete brothers would
get their hands dirty."

"they held up their end'a the bargain.
Bruno gone'n played his part
an' dispensed wit them quickly,"
I edged.

"did you kill them?"

Bruno spoke up
lookin' at Arlene through the rearview mirror
"most likely.
I ain't one t'take prisoners."

"then what would you consider
Johnny is in the trunk?"
Arlene insisted.

"collateral."

Her focused look on the road

was interrupted by a passin' cop
while her breathing increased
wit the steady rain that fell.

"relax darlin'
gonna be awhile b'fore they even know
who's missin' from there
an' we will be off the radar real soon,"
I encouraged.

"how can you be so certain?"

"you clearly don't know them Pete brothers very well.
they're gonna make it
so we don't even exist no more.
was easy fer them t'do it for themselves
imagine how much easier
it is fer them to make it so
for someone else?"

her grip on the steering wheel loosened
as she slid'r hand down t'the six o'clock position.
takin' a deep breath she continued
"I'm just so nervous, Michael.
I can't believe I just helped you escape prison!
what if we get caught?
are they going to kill us?
oh my God
I'm so scared now,"
she escalated her voice.

"relax, relax.
ev'rything's gonna be fine.
you gotta cool it
an' stay focused on the task at hand.
you said you were ready fer this.
there ain't no backin' out now," I enforced.

She was starting to fluster

so I had t'think my way in t'havin'
her think 'bout somethin' else.

"if you weren't a shrink
what would you have want'd t'be?"

she looked on at me briefly
seein' my demeanor an' attempt
at gettin' her t'think 'bout the question at hand
before she responded excitedly
"when I was a little girl
I always wanted to be an actress.
to be on TV or star in a film."

"so then why'd ya choose t'be a shrink?"
I pestered.

"well, honestly I just didn't think I was cut out
to be an actress.
my mother was a nurse and
she always had a knack for helping people.
I suppose you could say
her empathy rubbed off on me
and my will to help others
was stronger than my will to entertain them,"
she admitted.

CASE #127 - MICHAEL ENNIS (NOTES CONTINUED):

Michael apologized for his abrupt exit.
Told me the brothers had found the whereabouts of Michael's father.
Johnny took the letter and is torturing him with it.
Asked about his mother and father—said the story would be worth it.

I trust him.
I want to help him...

I was envious of actors and actresses.

afterall, they were the true deceivers in life.
imagine if you will
a life filled wit luxury
the feelin' of invincibility an' stardom.
where one puts on a face
that ain't even theirs
an' pretends t'be someone they ain't
strictly for the purpose of enjoyment.
the lies they tell themselves each day
t'fake a smile
t'fake a tear
t'fake a laugh
or fake distress.

they knew nothin' of the real world
its pleasures an' pains
b'cause they chose t'cover it up
wit all the things they faked.

But that was the difference

b'tween me and them.
I were fakin' b'cause that's the lie I lived
when the truth was but a fragment
of who I truly were on the inside
and on the out.

I'd endured my fair share of torture

no matter how you'd describe or define it.
an' like ev'ry man b'fore an' after
the ticket t'freedom is in its simplest form

hope.

when a man has hope, he has
undying
unyielding
an'
undeniable

power.

but hope can be misleadin'
an' that power can be drainin'
b'cause the diff'rence b'tween those
who want t'live
an' those who want t'survive
is what they're willin' to give.
an' if they ain't willin' t'give everything
t'sacrifice morals an' values and life
then they've already begun t'welcome

death.

"I understand that you are struggling

torn b'tween right an' wrong
inside this situation
you now find yerself in.
but I assure you
you are but using the one thing
that will always get in yer way—
yer heart.

my mother told me
t'keep the heart cold
b'cause it's easier t'warm it up.

when the heart is cold
it don't feel nothin'
b'cause feelings get in the way
of righteousness an' justice.

you may not see it that way
b'cause yer empathy blinds your way of thinkin'
but I told ya from the get-go
that your trust in me would pay off
an' we're so close t'witnessin' that,"
I stated eagerly.

"what would you have me do then?"
Arlene asked with concern.

"I'd have you be the thing you always wanted t'be—
an' actress.
t'fake concern an' hope for the man in the trunk.
he's only gonna give me what I want
if he thinks yer on his side
givin' him that single shred'a hope for escape."

"what makes you think that?"
Arlene tested.

"I know what hope does to a man
what it gives'm even in his most bleak moment.
he's gonna be desperate
an' my will is gonna be unwavering.
he's going t'see that right off the bat
that I'm not fuckin' around.
his time's gonna be limited
an' he's gonna give me what I want
b'cause insurance is the greatest commodity."

"I don't know if I can do it.
this is all so much right now.
why can't we just let him go
and run away together?
forget about everything
Johnny, the prison, your father…
we can just start a life together
you and me,"
she pleaded.

I stared out the sideview mirror

clenchin' my fist where Arlene wouldn't see
stretchin' the words an' reasons in my mind
the length of the distance we'd traveled
tryin' t'figure out how we got t'this moment
when days ago the plan was sketch'd
an' the pieces on the chess board placed
only t'now have it questioned and altered.

it weren't a matter of what was in my way
it was now a matter of what I had t'give away.

A piece of me

is but a mountain top
that thins the air
feelin' cold'n breezy
where I could freeze time itself
in a moment of forever.

an' so I gave her that moment
that one scrap of temptation
I knew would woo her
in t'my intentions.

"if ya truly love me
you'll help aid in my destiny
t'seek out the justice I deserve.
if you help me with this
I promise we will be t'gether
b'cause I love you,"
I confessed.

CASE #127 - MICHAEL ENNIS (NOTES CONTINUED):

I've chosen to help Michael in whatever plans he has.
He hasn't quite disclosed the whole plan but something is telling me to help him.
Why?
Am I falling for this man?
Am I helping to aid in a potential murder if he succeeds in killing his father?

He wants me to seduce Johnny so I can get the letter.

She reached over to my unclenched hand

interlockin' her fingers wit mine.
I could feel her resolve begin t'calm her
as she let out a small sigh
like a gentle gust'a wind
"okay, I'll do it
I'll help to give Johnny hope,"
she conceded.

We have to succumb to

the feelings we can nev'r fake
an' the common misconception is that
we can't fake love.

fake love is no diff'rent than a counterfeit bill:
at first
it's accepted
   it's honored
         its face value equal t'what it resembles.
at a second glance however
         its actual value is equivalent t'zero
   it's disgraceful
it's rejected.

Arlene were no different than any other
willingly acceptin' of the one thing she craved
yet unable t'tell the diff'rence
from what was real and what wasn't.
an' so I paid'r in full monetary value
of a feeling she had
an' a feeling I discarded.

The fool

is seldom the one fooling
the one who's easily fooled
regardless of how foolish their intentions are.

so it begs the question
'who was the fool?'

But like a snap of the finger

Arlene was back t'psychoanalysis
puttin' on her therapist shoes
drivin' t'wards the full understandin' of me.

"what are you going to do
when you finally confront your father?"
she asked eagerly.

Bruno spoke up
"how many times does the guy have t'say
kill'm b'fore ya understand that?"

"I know you're going to kill him.
but, are you going to declare who you are?
tell him what he did to you?
what you had to endure when he left you?"
she directed her questions t'me.

"don't suppose I've thought 'bout all that.
but surely he should know who I am
an' he knows what he done
but likely don't give'a shit
what happened t'me when he left.

he left b'cause he's a coward.
a no good piece of shit that deserves
ev'ry ounce of pain headed his way when we meet.
he will know who I am
without a doubt
b'cause he knows what he did
an' justice must be served."

"How are you comfortable with killing?"

Arlene asked fervently.

"you jus' gotta understand one thing:
on the inside
we're all comfortable with killin'.
on the outside
we just have t'become killers."

I gestured for her to turn

at the next road ahead of us
noticin' a dirt road leadin' t'wards a rail yard
"turn up here
this'll have t'do."

"we're only about 35 miles out
don't you think we should go further?"

"nah, we won't be long
an' we'll get more distance afterwards,"
I poised.

as Arlene started t'drive down the dirt road
my heart began t'race
feelin' the rich sense of excitement
pool beautiful thoughts of torture'n pain
that'd soon be displayed onto Johnny Boy
I couldn't help but flash'a smirk
that Arlene caught out the corner of'r eye.

"you're enjoying this aren't you?"

"life is full of simple pleasures
an' complex responses.
call this what ya want
but I assure you
the only thing that matters t'me
is what Johnny knows that I don't
an' I'm gonna not just enjoy
what I gotta do to extract that information
but bathe in the contentment."

All the pieces were in position.

the knights played.
the pawns almost all removed.
the queen in position.
the king soon cornered.

all that were left
was t'strike
hard'n swift
like a knife
that would change the course
of all things t'come.

We pulled in to a muddy patch

that had the vehicle slidin' a bit
but Arlene were able t'maneuver
makin' sure it didn't get stuck.
slammin' the car in t'park
she let the engine idle as she asked
"so how are we going to do this?"

"first, did ya get the knife I asked fer?"
she nodded yes.
"good.
so I'm gonna find a good place
t'tie Johnny up to.
Bruno will help me wit movin' him
an' if he gives any trouble
you go an' do that actin' stuff
like you wanna help'm don't forget.
I got an idea that'll make Johnny talk
nice'n quick.
you be on the lookout and jus' let Bruno'n I
take it all from here.
you done good darlin',"
I reached out an' pinched her chin.
and with a wink
I gave Arlene the last snapshot
of the man I chose fer her t'see.

Opening the trunk

Johnny's unconscious body barely looked t'be breathin'.
Bruno grabbed'm by the arm
an' slung his limp body ov'r his shoulder like a rifle.
humpin' his body t'where a nice rope contraption
could be utilized easiest
he dropped his body in a small puddle of mud
an' gazed up t'the sky
letting ant sized drops of rain pelt his face.

"it's time, Micheal.
time t'release the beast.
no more holdin' back
no more attachments
no more obstacles in our way.

you know what t'do."

Bruno handed me the knife he'd extracted
from the backseat of the car
I sheathed it in the back of my pants, statin'

"like I said from the get-go my friend
no person
no obstacle
nor emotion
gonna stop me
   from killin' my father."

CASE #127 - MICHAEL ENNIS (NOTES CONTINUED):

I'm going against everything I've learned as a psychologist.
I'm feeding into a man's delusions.
I'm helping a man escape prison.
I'm helping that same man potentially kill his own father.
I'm compelled to want him to succeed.

Is it so bad to want the bad guy to win?

RYAN A. KOVACS

THE NOTORIOUS MICHAEL ENNIS

The road was long

an' the journey unexpected
as ev'ry obstacle that came in my way
were overcome.

I spent years within the mentality of hate.
it were no longer a mindset
but a lifestyle
the drivin' force that
push'd at my back
an' pulled at my chest.

the past is dead.
there's no way t'revive it
no way t'relive it
an' no way t'receive it
and the pieces that were left b'hind in it.

you wanted t'know how this story began
an' now you'll know how it ends.

Bruno and I got in the car

after leavin' the last two bodies b'hind—
Arlene an' Johnny Boy.

knowin' the town we'd need t'get to
we drove like the devil were chasin' us
north in t'the heart of that small town
my father chose t'hide in.

like a rat
he feasted on the bottom
takin' scraps an' stealin' hearts
wit the sob stories he'd tell.
gettin' his free drinks
an' precious concerns
I'd rid the world of his presence.

and rest assured
while the very plan I had laid out
t'dispose of his soul
eradicating it from the plane of existence
I knew that the emptiness inside me
would not be filled wit his death
but it would be satisfying.

We pressed on

Bruno'n I
in t'the small town
where bars reeked of his breath.

constantly bein' one step b'hind it felt like
we scoured the town in under a week
fillin' in the gaps of prime time drinkin'
an' constantly searchin' fer the face of a grainy picture.

with money we stole from passersby
an' drunk oafs at each bar
we managed t'stay afloat
hidin' out in a cheap motel
that never once said our name.

the Pete brothers made good on their promise
an' in time I'd be makin' good on mine.

but that's when it happened.

no sooner did the thought cross my mind
standin' idly outside a corner store
wit Bruno'n I smokin' our evening cigs
the promise I swore t'uphold
was the glimpse I'd been lookin' for.

Bruno saw just as I did

the man from the picture
who'd stuck out like a red dot
on a black'n white picture.

an' that's precisely what I saw—
the color red.

blindin' me
surroundin' me
swallowin' me whole
like a whale eatin' krill
my body tensed from the
thrill t'kill.

Bruno grabbed my shoulder

his eyes wide like a predator 'bout t'strike

"this is it.
that's him,"
he glanced once more at the folded picture.
"no mercy.
no fuckin' mercy.
this is the man you've sworn to kill.

now kill'm."

As I approached the man

the thought of course cross'd my mind
whether or not he was the man I'd sworn t'kill.

the picture the brothers gave me
certainly looked like my father
but I had to ask myself
could I have been deceived as easily as Arlene
bein' blinded by the one thing I craved?
I never dared t'question the truth b'hind
the two men who swore t'help me
and did ev'rything they could t'make sure I escaped.
it begged to question all the things I never thought 'bout:

why didn't the brothers want t'come wit me?
why did they choose t'remain there?
was I killin' someone fer them rather than my actual father?

the promise I'd made t'them sounded too simple—
t'spread propaganda…
an' that were it.
did they even care about that
or was this man they possibly led me on t'believin' were my father
someone they wanted dead?

the brothers knew ev'rything I was lookin' fer
yet I had no clue what they were lookin' for
when quite possibly I were it.
they saw me
hell bent'n driven t'succeed
that they filled my mind wit nonsense
leading me on t'believe that this man
was indeed my father
when I possibly didn't even know.

the paranoia started t'fuck wit my head
an' sometimes the simplest answer is to act.
so I did.

They say

the human heart is made outta love
that inside resides them fuzzy feelin's
an' emotions
where joy'n desire'n affection are built up
by those that surround us
bringin' them feel-good chemicals t'the brain
like'a drug we nev'r tried b'fore.

but I'm here t'tell ya
the heart can be made of hate.
it can be chiseled from rock
formed from obsidian
draped in ice that never melts.
it can be numbed
an' lifeless like a corpse on'a table.
it can be sewn'n stitch'd an' stapled
beaten, bludgeoned'n left fer dead.
the heart can be
ripped out
torn out
worn out
or straight up broken

but not mine.

I've learned how t'live wit this
organ in my body
that once was fragile
an' now is indestructible.

"Keep the heart cold because it's easier to warm it up"

were the last words my mother spoke t'me
the day she died
right b'fore I gone'n killed her myself.

in that moment I had no fuckin' clue what that meant
nor could I fathom what it'd mean t'me now.

when I first analyzed the phrase
I noticed how cold it made me feel.
naturally of course I should'a felt cold
since that's what she stated
but I had to question
why?
why cold?
why not just be cold t'wards those
who don't fill my heart wit love?
why have a cold heart all t'gether?

I'll tell you why.
because people are vicious.
they are teeth snarlin' animals.
they are blood suckin' leeches.
they are bottomless pits'a self pity an' hypocrisy.
they are soulless beings held t'gether by flesh and bone.
they are hopeless'n helpless having only one similarity

they will all die.

and that is what warms my heart.

You see

if ya wanna be a killer
you can't have any attachments
can't have pity or remorse.
ya gotta press on like yer fightin' fer your life
as a gladiator would.
there's the now'n the then
'cause the future ain't guaranteed
unless you make it so.

took me a few years t'figure it out
but after my first taste'a blood
that day on the baseball diamond
the remainin' string attached t'my heart
was severed like that bird's head
when I realized how important it truly were
t'not have emotions
an' t'bury them feelin's so far down
my core would burn them up
wit the fire burnin' in my soul.

sure I mourned fer that less'r creature
but it taught me that valuable lesson
my mother never explained in detail
b'fore her passing
that with'a cold heart
I wouldn't have t'feel anything—
nev'r have the fear of bein' let down or disappointed.
a cold heart would grant me access t'those
whose hearts were already warm
where I could penetrate them an' use them
an' discard them like waste.
if I learned t'keep my heart cold
I'd never need t'warm it up again.

an' I never did.

When I killed that bird

I killed Michael Ennis.
he was weak
he was afraid
he was insecure.

he needed t'be changed
needed t'be more
and thus I were reborn as

                                                    Bruno.

CASE #127 - MICHAEL ENNIS (NOTES CONTINUED):

Suspicions of molestation and sexual abuse were right (by uncle).
Won't budge on what happened to his mother.
Asked about Bruno again (still haven't seen him over past few months).
Dissociative identity disorder possible?
Bruno and Michael have been friends since they were teenagers.
Bruno doesn't have a father.
Michael came bursting in my office after our session.
Declared he was Bruno.

Michael IS Bruno...

With a new identity

I could be whoev'r I desired
an' not fear consequences like a child would.
I needed a plan
somethin' t'motivate me
an' keep me goin' no matter what.

if I were heartless over'a bird
findin' the epiphany I'd longed fer
since my mother's passing
I knew I'd have t'be willin' to kill anyone
'cause I was sure as hell willin'
t'kill my father.

So I had to justify everything

no matter what it cost me.
ev'rything placed b'fore me
each obstacle an' task
was but a steppin' stone in the direction
of killin' the man
who'd help bring me in t'this world
an' I'd help him leave it.

thus my rampage began.

Killing my uncle

who whipped me
beat me
an' forced himself on me sexually
found his actions t'be displeasing
before I shot him in the head
wit his own Colt .45.
     justified.

Killing my uncle's whore

who chose to overlook
my uncle's unorthodox behavior
yet pretended t'care like'a mother would
found out that her insides matched her outsides
when I tied her to her lover
b'fore she gone'n bled out.
                    justified.

Killing Johnny Boy

the man who'd stepped in front of me
constantly bein' the thorn in my side
preventin' me from completing each small task
that'd bring me closer t'the only moment I craved.
his actions brought on his pain
when he were nev'r part of the original plan
but made himself a sacrificial pawn
the moment he cross'd me.
justified.

Killing Arlene

the gal that made it all happen
who dropped the hints an' played the game
thinkin' I were the king
protectin' me like some bear
safeguardin' its cub.
she met the monster
found out he wasn't who he claimed t'be
but dared t'take away my vengeance
dared t'question my reasons
an' be the righteous one in the eyes of justice.
she met her end when she tried t'penetrate my heart
and found out there was nothin' there.
                                    justified.

Killing my father

the man who stood b'fore me
as my eyes locked wit his
we each retraced the footsteps t'the present
where we had come from
that brought us t'that moment.

an' in that moment
I felt the lord an' the devil
walk in my soul
each pullin' in a diff'rent direction
each whisperin' their commands
each shoutin' the repercussions
each absent from what I had believed

that in a single fragment of time
I were the epitome
of my name.

CASE #127 - MICHAEL ENNIS (NOTES CONTINUED):

Trauma induced dissociative identity disorder present.
Michael told me how his father tricked him into killing his own mother.
I see his intensions much clearer now.
His father must die for his crime.
We are going to do it together.

I love him.

I stood

tremblin' with anticipation
while blood boiled in my body
bubblin' over like a tea kettle
screaming from the heat.
tunnel vision lurked in steadily
then quickly, like a dart on a bullseye
as my body tensed wit rage'n fury
while I started t'wards the man
who took ev'rything from me.

My legs

pumped like oil rigs in a desert
pulsatin' muscle fibers that twitched wit anticipation
as my inner voice bellowed like that of a warrior
makin' his last stand 'gainst an army of hordes.

I moved wit purpose an' intent
t'wards the enemy I saw fit to destroy
running at him like a juggernaut
unable t'be stopped or tamed
drivin' my knee into his quadricep
paralyzing him as he fell to the rocky dirt.

his scream was incoherent t'me
while I displayed my malleable actions upon his body
sinkin' my foot deep into his ribcage
stealin' the breath right from his lungs.

My hands

wrapped tightly like an anaconda
grippin' the back of his neck
draggin' him t'his feet
and slammin' him onto the hood of the nearest car.
when he tried to flail an' weasel his way from my grasp
I swatted his hands away like a pesky fly
all while pummeling his battered face.

bloody an' bludgeoned
his yells turned t'grumbles
an' his grumbles turned t'whimpers
as my hammer-like fists flattened his body
like metal on an anvil.

My skin

crawled'n itch'd fer more
hungered to bathe in his agony
like the ichor that flowed through mythological beings
with unquenchable thirst for slaughter.

smearing his blood b'tween
the cracks'n crevices'n pores of my hands an' arms
I soaked my body in gore
of the lust for murder
crushing any hope of survival for the man
who taught me the meaning of enduring pain'n sufferin'.

My jaw

clenched an' ground my teeth
while my gums collapsed under pressure
wit saliva buildin' up under my tongue
seething an' foamin' at my mouth.
spit began t'spew onto his limp body
like I were a dog hot on a scent—

the scent of death.

smellin' it an' tastin' it in the back of my throat
I gulped
heaving air into my lungs with each blow
I brought down on his corpse.

My chest

expanded to that of the size of the universe
as I exhaled one final time
wit the last blow landed
upon his rigid figure.

I hadn't even noticed
how I'd mounted his waist on the hood'a the car
pinning him down like nails on a cross
with his feet barely danglin' off the bumper
arms laid out like a two by four
an' his face completely unrecognizable
flattened an' meshed with the blue paint
makin' it purple in hue.

I breathed heavily
my sight gradually widening
witnessin' the carnage that fell around me
with blank stares an' shocked faces
of the men'n women who gazed at me.

screams became repetitive
while others ran t'wards phones an' safety
callin' authorities
with demands for my arrest.

I was a man

jus' like any other man
the one they'd call legend
the one they'd call an imposter
the one they'd soon have lock'd up once more.

but it didn't bother me none
b'cause you don't make a name
when a name makes you.

my goal was achieved
justice had been served
as cold an' valid as it could ever be.

I killed my father
jus' as I promised.

and that didn't make me the enemy.

no

that made me

        Notorious.

EPILOGUE

After I killed my father

I sought out the nearest bar
knowin' damn well it were but a matter of time
b'fore the cops showed up
t'take me down an' lock me up once more.
but commemoration were in order
t'celebrate my victory
an' honor those who helped pave the way
with their corpses
of the destruction I had created.

the bartender stared at me in bewilderment
likely questionin' the manner in which I presented myself
wit blood splatter on my shirt'n pants
caked underneath my fingernails
an' smudged along my arms'n face
I gestured t'him fer the bottle of gin on the shelf.
he looked at the blue bottle
then turned t'me and asked
"rough day?"

"got jumped in the alley.
had t'show them boys who they were messin' wit."

concerned, the bartender stated
"looks like you showed them rascals.
here, first shot is on me.
for your troubles."
he poured the shot
with liquid touching the rim of the glass.
how fortuitous it had been
that I was given the momentous opportunity
to quote the man
I'd just killed
who always notoriously said
"non mea culpa hoc potu sum."

Just as I put the glass to my mouth

feelin' the pleasant liquor warm my lips
a hand placed itself on my shoulder
like a forgotten friend reintroducing themselves
while a whisper in my ear echoed like waves on the ocean
crashin' on me like the weight of the world

"that's my line."

ACKNOWLEDGEMENTS

I'd like to thank my editor, Lois Taubman, for her advice on how to make this book a published piece of literature; my High School English teacher, Mrs. VanLare, for teaching me the value of contributing a verse to society; And last, I thank my father, who wrote a quote on a napkin when I was 14 years old in a Chinese restaurant that read, *"Anything you sincerely believe in, ardently desire, and enthusiastically act upon, will inevitably come to pass."*

ABOUT THE AUTHOR

RYAN A. KOVACS is a Rochester, NY native who loves to travel, meet new people and have profound conversations. His writing stems from his many experiences and the diverse spectrum of personalities he's encountered over the years. Poetry is what moves him, and his true talent lies in storytelling. His first published book is titled *I Considered You*, which he followed up with *The N.M.E.*, both novels in verse. Ryan served in the United States Army and continues to serve in the Air National Guard. He is a family man who surrounds himself with like-minded people, and has never been one to shy away from uncomfortable topics. Give him a beer and he'll provide the storytelling.